JAMBOREE JUSTICE

A MAGICAL MANE MYSTERY
BOOK SEVEN

STELLA BIXBY

FERRY TAIL PUBLISHING LLC

This novel is a work of fiction. Names, characters, places, and incidents are either a product of the author's imagination or are used fictitiously. Any resemblance to actual persons, living or dead, businesses, events, or locales is entirely coincidental.

Copyright © 2022 by Crystal S. Ferry

All rights reserved.

No part of this book may be reproduced or transmitted in any form or by any means, electronic or mechanical, including photocopying, recording, or by any information storage and retrieval system presently available or yet to be invented without permission in writing from the publisher, except for the use of brief quotations in a book review.

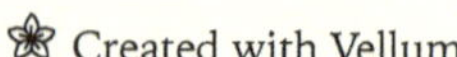 Created with Vellum

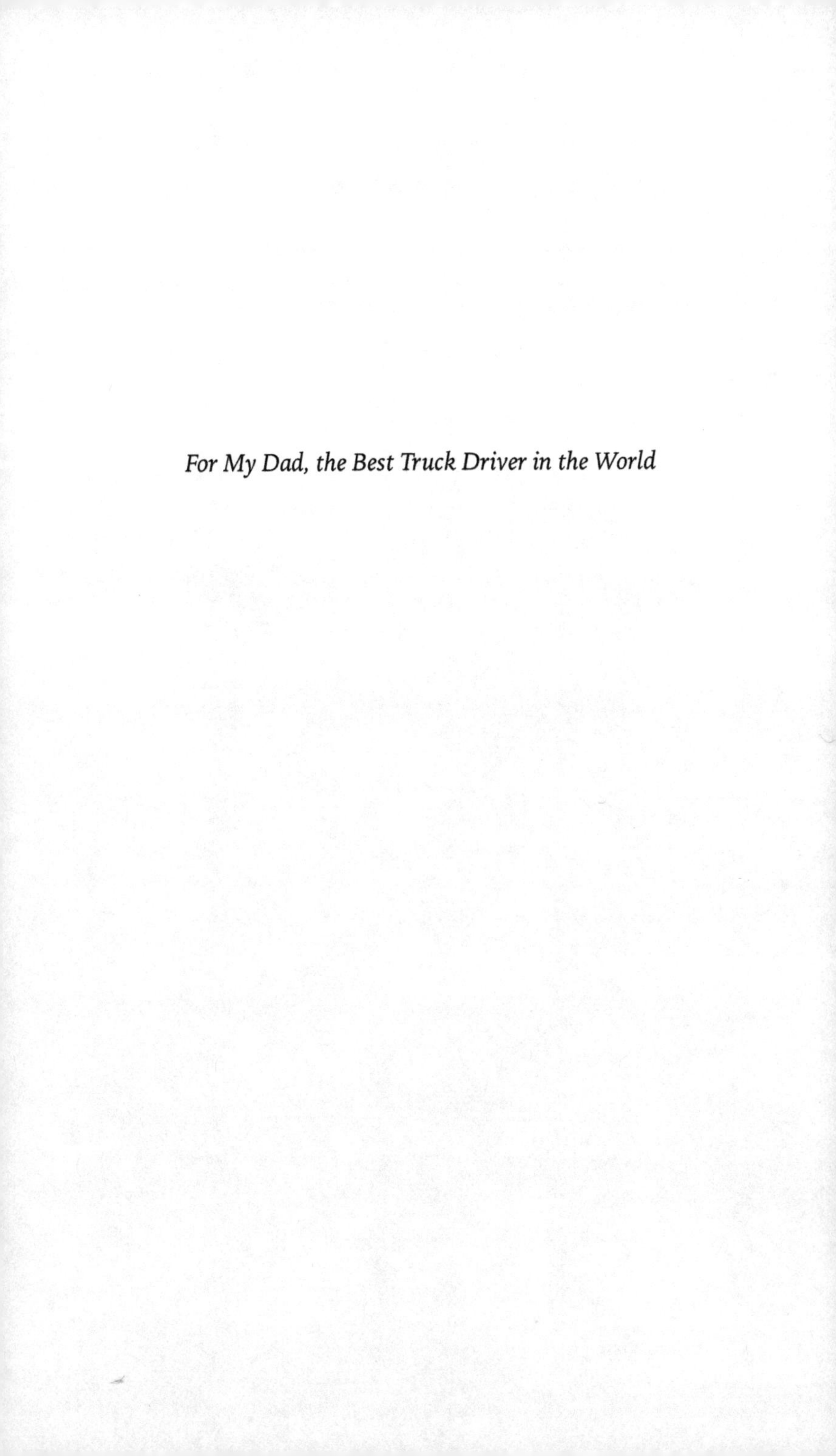

For My Dad, the Best Truck Driver in the World

CAST OF CHARACTERS

Ellie - Main Character

Penelope - Ellie's Pet Pig

Mona - Ellie's VW Microbus

Esme - Ellie's Grandmother

Emily/Miley - Ellie's Mother

Xander - Warlock

Jake - Cliff Haven Police Chief/Emily's High School Sweetheart

Bex - Ellie's Best Friend/Works at Katie's Café

Katie - Married to Earl/Own's Katie's Café & Theater

Fran - Coupled with Amy/Own's Fran's Fabric & Feed

Amy - Coupled with Fran/Own's Amy's Antiques

Nancy - Married to Hank/Own's Nancy's Nails

Renée - Widowed/Grand Witch of the States

Andrea - Ellie's Magical Guardian

Gerald - Xander's Father

Randy - Owner of Jubilant Jewel Jamboree & Trucking Company

Gar - Randy's Ex-Wife and Business Partner
Stacie - Randy's Fiancée
KayLynn - Randy's Girlfriend
Bridget - Randy's Girlfriend

IN THE LAST BOOK . . .

In *Festival Fiasco*, the previous book in the Magical Mane Mystery Series, Ellie had to figure out who murdered her magical cousin—the one who had been trying to kill her.

Ellie solved the case and returned to her barn where the mural had changed to a diner. Ellie touched a speck of magic and was transported only to see Emily, her mother, waiting tables inside the diner.

Much to Ellie's surprise, Xander walked out of the diner in a way that seemed like he and Emily were good friends, if not more.

Xander got on his motorcycle and turned toward Ellie. She panicked and transported herself back to the barn.

Continue her story in *Jamboree Justice* by turning the page!

The diner taunted my memory. I'd fall asleep thinking about it, dream about it, and wake up exhausted from seeing my mother.

Not to mention, Xander walking out waving as if he and Emily were the best of friends. He promised he'd tell me when he found her.

He lied.

I spent my days in front of the mural, hoping it would change. My magic wouldn't take me back to the diner, no matter how hard I tried.

If it hadn't been for my best friend and pet pig, Penelope, I probably wouldn't have left the couch in my barn studio.

She nudged my leg for the first time today and oinked softly at me.

"Are you hungry, sweetheart?"

She spun in a circle at my feet. If only I could garner as much enthusiasm as she had or as much of an appetite.

"Popcorn with peanut butter?"

This made her squeal jovially.

I smiled, and my face felt funny. It wasn't an expression I'd worn in a while.

Sure, my friends checked in on me regularly, though none of those friends were Xander.

I was convinced he'd seen me standing on the other side of the road when he'd pulled out of the diner on his motorcycle. Why else would he be avoiding me?

Bernardo, Xander's cousin, had to return to Argentina soon after the Strawberry Festival, but I didn't care much. It wasn't like I would tell him what I'd seen. I wouldn't tell anyone. Not until I knew it wasn't just some figment of my imagination.

I pushed myself off the couch and stretched. I hadn't done yoga in more than a month, with the stiffness in my muscles to prove it.

The mural and the couch were at the back of my barn that the Cliff Haven residents had helped me turn into an exercise studio. As I pushed past the curtain separating the studio from the mural, I did my best not to notice the dust collecting on the equipment or the lack of shine on the polished wood floor.

The air was muggy and hot, with the sun high in the sky. "Penelope, you must be starving. I had no idea it was practically noon."

She let out a small grunt.

"Next time, tell me sooner," I said, scooping her up off the ground and nuzzling into her neck. "Silly girl."

She squealed with delight.

Like the mural, my house was magical. Practically everything in my life was magical. Not that I'd known this very long. I mean, I knew my hair changed colors and shapes when my emotions flared, but otherwise, I'd been in the dark.

In less than a year, I'd gone from entirely clueless about the magical world to next in line to be the Grand Witch of the States—a title that transferred through my family bloodlines.

And since Emily was nowhere to be found—other than when I saw her through the mural at the diner—I was it.

I glanced around, half-expecting to see my grandmother's ghost floating in the kitchen, but she wasn't there. I guess I lied before when I said I hadn't told anyone. She knew I'd seen Emily. Emily was her daughter, after all. Plus, she'd been there when I'd gone into the mural.

But since that night, I'd only seen her a handful of times, and most of the time, it was from a distance.

I did my best not to feel abandoned by my family for the millionth time in my life. Though, I'd probably have those feelings forever, as I grew up in multiple foster homes after Emily left me at a fire station when I was an infant.

Only one bag of popcorn lay on the shelf in the pantry. I'd scraped the massive jar of peanut butter clean, meaning I'd have to venture into town to get groceries soon.

One thing about my friends was they only coddled for so long. Being mothers and grandmothers themselves, they did their fair share of coddling when I'd first fallen into my funk, but now they'd stopped bringing me groceries and meals. They were just trying to get me out of the house, but I didn't have to like it.

"Looks like we'll be making a trip to town," I said as the bag of popcorn popped in the microwave.

Penelope looked up at me like I'd just admitted that I secretly turned into a werewolf every night.

"I mean, I'll have to go into town," I said. "It's too hot for you to stay in Mona while I go into the store. But if you're going to eat, I'll have to go."

Penelope oinked loudly in agreement.

If only I knew what she was trying to say.

We were very connected—had been since I'd gotten her—but lately, my connection to everything seemed shaky.

The microwave's beep sounded as the smell of butter and salty deliciousness wafted through the kitchen. I quickly added the last of the peanut butter to the fluffy white kernels and set the bowl on the floor for Penelope to enjoy.

She looked up at me as if to tell me to have some.

"I'm okay," I said. "Not very hungry."

Penelope hesitated only a second before diving in. She had to be starving. I hadn't fed her since the night before, and she was used to getting three solid meals.

I needed to get my head in a better space. I wasn't just responsible for myself. I was responsible for my sweet piglet, too.

Maybe I was focusing too much on seeing my mom. Maybe if I let it go for a while, everything would work itself out.

"Do I smell popcorn?" Andrea—my magical guardian, kind of like the secret service agents of the magical world—asked when she walked in the back door. It looked like she'd just been on a run, which was entirely likely.

She'd been doing a lot of working out since becoming my guardian. She said it kept her mind from going numb watching me do nothing all day.

"That's all we have," I said, motioning to the bowl Penelope was almost finished gobbling down. "I'm going to the store this afternoon to get some more."

"That's great news," she said, her voice serious as usual. "I'll shower and go with you."

I hopped off the stool at the island. "I need to shower, too. Meet you down here in a bit."

Andrea didn't technically live with me, but she stayed every once in a while, meaning she made herself at home. Which was perfectly fine with me. My home was so large it could house tons of people.

I hurried up the stairs, and Penelope's little feet came charging after me.

"Don't come up," I said, turning back to her. "I'll be right back. You eat."

She looked up at me from the bottom of the grand wooden staircase, hesitated, then turned and went back to her popcorn.

I always loved the corridor at the top of the stairs. Several doors lined the hallway—each leading to a room with its own personality. When I'd first arrived at the house after getting a letter from my deceased grandmother, Esme, I'd tried to sleep in every room.

None of the beds were comfy enough to get any shut-eye. So I'd ended up back in Mona, my VW Microbus, sleeping in the bed I was most used to. Until I finally allowed myself to sleep in Esme's room. The one with the lilac flower wreath on the door that never wilted.

I'd never gotten a better night of sleep in my life.

The flower wreath was glorious in its purple hues this morning, almost as if it knew I was coming.

The attached bathroom was spotless. In fact, the entire house was spotless now that I thought about it. I could not use my magic to clean yet, but I knew a few people who did. Though, those people hadn't visited in a while.

I shrugged it away. The house was mysterious. It had more magic than I could fathom.

The hot water felt delightful in my hair. I'd pulled it into a severe bun days ago and hadn't even checked to see if it had changed. But as I shampooed and conditioned it, the dull gray faded, and colors flickered to life.

After struggling with it my entire life, I'd finally figured out how to control the changes. Now, when I was sad, mad, happy, or scared, I could keep my hair from going into a frizzy orange ball or dark purple ringlets or long French braids.

But as I finished up my shower, I let the magic flow through every strand, letting them come to life. And as they did, my heart lifted. My inner being wasn't so heavy, and my head felt clearer.

Before I headed to town, there was somewhere I needed to go first.

2

Inside the small hole in the bottom of my bedroom wall, a button released a latch to reveal a hidden staircase behind a large bookshelf. Small lights cast a golden glow on the curved wooden staircase as I walked up the spiral stairs.

The attic was as I'd left it, which was as Esme had left it before she died. The large armchair sat in the middle with a small table next to it. A journal and a pen were the only items on the table. The journal had been Esme's, but I'd added my own notes to the back pages when the journal prompted.

Like everything else in the house, the journal was magical. It only revealed what it wanted me to know. Or what Esme wanted me to know.

I sat in the chair, pulling my legs up and crossing them. My hair flowed down my shoulders in sparkly iridescent waves.

As I flipped through the journal, waiting to find a new page in a language I could read, I hummed a little tune.

When I reached the pages I'd written, I flipped back, but the journal gripped its previous pages together.

"Going forward, okay," I said as I flipped through what I'd written. "Do I need to write today?"

I reached for the pen on the table, but just as my fingers almost grasped it, it fell off the table.

"Okay, so no writing," I said with a laugh.

I flipped to the last of my entries and stopped.

"Is this it?"

If I had seen myself talking to a journal a year ago, I would have thought I'd gone crazy.

But the journal responded in its own way, flipping the pages to reveal another entry—one not made by me.

My heart raced in my chest. It was Esme's writing, and it was fresh.

My Dearest Ellie,

If you see this, you've come out the other side and have found your will again.

You may have noticed I have been around very little lately. I will explain later. Please know it's not because I don't want to talk to or be with you. I simply have something very important I'm working on, and your energy these past few weeks has been draining.

Now that you're back, I will surely see you soon.

Keep up the good energy.

Love,

Esme

Tears stung at the corners of my eyes. I didn't know my negative energy could drain someone else's. Especially a ghost's.

I brushed away the feeling. I would do everything I could not to sink back into the pit of despair. From now on, I wanted my attitude only to attract good energy.

I closed the journal and replaced it on the table before heading back down the stairs.

Penelope greeted me in my bedroom with big, round eyes.

"What's wrong?" I asked.

She tugged at my pant leg, pulling me toward the

stairs. I carried her down. Pigs have a harder time going down the stairs than up because of how their legs function.

"Everything's going to be okay," I said. "I have my energy back. My hair is back. My magic is back. We don't need to find my mother. Life here in Cliff Haven is perfect. I'll call the ladies and get them over here after Andrea, and I go to town."

Penelope oinked and glanced up at the back door off the kitchen.

I looked to see the exact women I'd just said I would call. Katie, Nancy, Fran, Amy, and Renée stood with horrible looks on their faces.

"What happened?" I asked. "Why do you look like someone died?"

"Someone did die," Renée—the temporary Grand Witch of the States—said. "And your mother is the prime suspect."

3

I sank onto a bar stool, letting Penelope down to the floor. My scalp tingled, and my hair that had been so prettily draped down my shoulders was now tightening into a bun on top of my head. I let it.

"You found my mother?" I asked.

"I did," Renée said. "I was on my way to tell you when I got word of the murder."

"And they think my mother is the killer? Emily Vander-wick?" I asked.

"She doesn't go by that name anymore," Renée said.

Katie moved to my side and rubbed my back.

"What do you mean she doesn't go by her real name?" I asked though I knew the minute I asked the question was silly.

"If she'd gone by her real name, we would have located her long before now," Renée answered, thankfully not using a condescending tone. "She calls herself Miley Mulroney."

I gasped.

"She used Jake's last name," Katie said.

"And Miley is just an anagram of Emily," I said. "How have we not found her?"

Renée shook her head. "I'm not sure. But we will get to the bottom of it."

Nancy bustled around the kitchen, looking through the cupboards. Her red outfit was on point and showed off her many tattoos. She was the summer version of a tattooed Mrs. Claus.

"Is Emily—or Miley—in jail?" I asked.

"They haven't completely processed the crime scene, but her name has been floating around with the investigators."

Nancy turned to me and interrupted. "You have nothing in your cupboards. No wonder you're so skinny. You're not eating."

"I was just about to head to the store with Andrea," I said. "I haven't been hungry."

My stomach growled as if in protest.

"We don't have time to eat, anyway," Renée said.

Nancy rolled her eyes behind Renée's back.

"We need to get to that crime scene so you can work your magic—not your actual magic, but your crime-solving magic—and find out who killed that man before they take your mom to jail." Renée started toward the door.

"Where are we going?" Andrea asked, coming down the stairs.

"We have to help my mom get out of some legal trouble," I said. "Do you want to come?"

Andrea looked at Renée, then back at me. "Of course, I want to come. I have to come. It's my job."

"Okay, let's go then," I said. "Penelope, you should probably stay here."

"Bring her," Renée said. "She might be helpful."

I didn't object.

"We're coming too," Katie said.

"No," Renée said. "There's not enough room."

"There is in Mona," Nancy said. "Come on. We can help."

The others gave Renée their best puppy dog faces.

"Fine," Renée said. "But you cannot speak to Emily. If she recognizes you, we don't know how she'll react. We've only just found her, and we don't want to lose her again."

"I can't speak to her either?" I asked.

Renée gave me a sad nod. "I'm sorry. No. Not yet, anyway. Not until we get everything sorted."

We walked out into the muggy afternoon, and my friends piled into Mona's side door, with Renée taking the front seat.

I went to the driver's side, but it was locked.

I tapped on the window, and Renée leaned over to unlock the door, but she couldn't get it to budge.

I pulled on the handle again, but it burned my hand this time.

"Mona," I said. "Are you mad at me?"

I could have sworn I heard a slight grumble come from her non-running engine.

"I'm sorry I haven't been out to visit lately," I said. "I've been in a funk. But I'm back now. I promise I will never leave you to sit again for so long."

I tried the handle, this time more carefully, and it opened.

"Thank you." I slid into the front seat. "Is everyone situated back there?"

The back of my van was more of a living space than a passenger space.

The five women crowded together on the bed, Penelope in between them.

"Good as we'll ever be," Katie said.

Renée let out a little sigh.

"Where are we going?" I asked.

"Denver," Renée said.

"Denver, Iowa?" I asked.

"Denver, Colorado."

"You're telling me my mother has been in Colorado this entire time?"

I'd grown up in Colorado—gone from foster home to foster home in Colorado—and Emily had been there all along?

"We'll figure everything out," Renée said. "But first, we have to solve this crime. If your mother goes to jail, we may never know what she's been up to the past twenty-some years."

I resisted the urge to let my emotions take over. I wouldn't bring draining energy to those around me. Especially not Renée—the woman in charge of all the witches and warlocks in the United States.

"Anywhere specific in Denver?" I asked. "Or just Denver?"

"We need to go to the open convention center," Renée said. "To the Jubilant Jewel Jamboree."

"What is a Jubilant Jewel Jamboree?" I asked.

"You'll see when we get there."

I tickled Mona's dash. "Mona, will you please take us to the Jubilant Jewel Jamboree in Denver at the open convention center?"

Before I finished asking my question, we were hurtling off into space with the women in the back of the van—minus Andrea—screaming at the top of their lungs.

"Would you quiet down?" Renée asked.

"Why are we going so fast?" Nancy yelled, holding onto the counter with the tiny sink.

"How else are we supposed to get there before Emily—Miley—gets arrested?" Renée asked.

Mona slowed to a stop, and my ears popped.

"See?" Renée asked. "Much faster than an airplane."

"You mean to tell me we're already in Denver, Colorado?" Katie asked with a scoff.

"Take a look for yourself," Renée said. "And drink some water. The quick change in altitude can mess with people."

Mona's door slid open, revealing the Denver skyline with picturesque mountains behind it.

Part of me exhaled. This might not be my forever home, but it had been home once, and I loved it.

"If you look to your right, you'll see the Jubilant Jewel Jamboree." Renée motioned like a game show host showing off a prize pack.

I expected to see some sort of amusement park or festival like the one we'd had in Cliff Haven not too long before.

Instead, my eyes landed on rows and rows of shiny colorful semi-trucks.

"This is where my mom is?" I asked.

"This is where the dead man is," Renée said. "Who knows where your mother is?"

4

I f I had to guess, there were probably close to five thousand people scattered around the massive open-air convention center, which looked like a glorified parking lot with permanent vendor tents, rows of port-o-potties, and a large wooden canopy structure with a food and beverage sign on top.

"Where did they find the dead man?" I asked.

"Follow me," Renée said, walking toward the food pavilion. "You probably won't be able to get close to him. There are tons of police officers."

"How long ago did he die?" I asked.

"Not sure," Renée said. "The police have been here since this morning."

"We'll distract the police," Katie said.

Renée let out a psh sound.

"What?" Katie asked. "You don't think these old ladies can distract a couple of handsome police officers?"

Renée, smartly, didn't reply.

When we reached the side of the pavilion, the police

had already strung police tape between the poles. Katie, Nancy, Amy, and Fran huddled like a football team.

Renée looked exasperated, but I didn't have time to play moderator.

I looked around, trying to take in any information I could. The body seemed to be in the kitchen area of one of the food stalls inside the pavilion.

He could have been a chef or a dishwasher, though, from the looks of the bright blue snakeskin cowboy boots poking out the door, he was likely neither. Those were not the shoes someone wore to stand in a kitchen all day.

I saw no blood, but a puddle of water had settled under the boots. Evidence could have been lost if the body had been drenched in water. I cringed.

"Ready, break," Katie said, and the others clapped once.

They flew into action.

Fran and Amy walked directly toward the crime scene, stumbling over one another, acting like they were drunk.

They pushed past the police tape with loud laughter.

This drew two of the five police officers away from the scene as they scolded Fran and Amy for messing with a crime scene.

Then Katie flopped to the ground.

I gasped and rushed toward her, but she looked up and winked.

Ah, this was part of the plan.

The delayed scream that came out of her mouth sounded like what a cat would sound like if someone stepped on its tail.

Nancy started screaming for help as she carefully lowered herself to the ground next to Katie.

Two more police officers ran over to help them.

Which left one.

The scary-looking one.

I glanced at Andrea and Renée to see if they had any ideas.

Renée pulled her phone out of her pocket and checked a text. "I have to go. You better get in there quickly if you want to see the crime scene."

"But how?"

"You'll figure it out," she hurried away, leaving me all alone.

I could use my magic to transport me inside the kitchen area, but if I depleted my magic and they found me in there, they'd freak out.

"Don't use magic," Andrea said. "I can handle him."

"Are you sure?"

"Get in, take your pictures, and get out," she said. "No dawdling."

The crowd was thick but didn't extend to the police line. Everyone had probably already gotten their photos and moved on with their lives. A few hours-old crime scene was practically yesterday's news. It was almost sad, in a way.

When I glanced over to see Andrea, she was gone.

Katie and Nancy had their officers' attention, as did Amy and Fran. When I caught sight of Andrea, she was in a full-blown argument with the scary-looking officer. I couldn't let their hard work go to waste.

I sucked in a breath and hurried toward the scene.

I heard Andrea and the officer's argument as I got closer.

"I have a right to know if it's my father," Andrea yelled. "He's been missing for days."

"Like I already told you," the officer yelled back in a booming voice. "File a missing person's report with the police department. We'll notify next of kin when we can."

Andrea didn't even flinch. She continued to yell.

I ducked under the tape and slipped through the doorway.

I used my camera app on my phone to snap pictures of the dead man dressed in full cowboy garb, complete with a big black hat that seemed to have been placed over his face and a blue-handled kitchen steak knife stuck in the middle of his chest.

I lifted the water-logged hat with the slightest touch to the side of the brim so I didn't leave fingerprints—though I didn't know if they could even get fingerprints off of soggy felt—then took a good shot of his face.

I tried to photograph all the different angles.

The body was soaked, and the dishwasher sprayer seemed to be the tool used. It wasn't attached to the little hook at the back of the sink to keep it out of the way, almost as if someone had turned the water on, sprayed the body, turned it off, then left.

Besides the knife in his chest, I saw no bruising or blood. His fingernails were clean, and big gold rings circled almost all his fingers.

This wasn't a robbery gone bad.

"You can't go in there," Andrea's panicked voice came from the doorway.

"Don't tell me where I can and cannot go," a man I suspected was the scary-looking officer said. "If you don't get out of here right now, I'll have you arrested."

I was trapped.

I couldn't get out of the small kitchen unless I went through the tiny windows where they took orders and put the food trays through. I might have lost some weight, but I wasn't small enough to manage that.

The food prep station was my only hope. I ducked under the counter behind a trashcan, careful not to touch anything or leave fingerprints.

Boots stomped around—two pairs.

"Any update on Miley Mulroney?" the scary officer asked.

"Nothing," another officer replied. "Everyone says the diner just didn't open this morning. She's the one with the keys. My guess is she stabbed him, hosed him down, and hit the road. She could be anywhere by now."

They were right. Why would I have assumed that we'd even see her here?

Because I didn't think she was the killer, that's why. She had no reason to run. But the fact that she didn't show up for work was strange. Or maybe not. I knew nothing about her. She could have been incredibly unreliable for all I knew.

"Amazingly, there isn't any other evidence," the scary officer said. "Are you sure the crime scene team checked everywhere? Maybe something rolled behind the trashcan."

My body froze. If they moved the trashcan, they'd find

me. I'd go to jail, and any hope of me getting my mom off the hook for this murder was out the window.

I closed my eyes and willed myself to teleport, but nothing happened. It had been so long since I'd used my magic in any actual capacity. Renée once explained to me how magic was like a muscle—you had to use it to keep it in shape.

Trying to teleport right now would be like going on a five-mile run after not lacing up my running shoes in the last month.

My scalp tingled, and my hair twisted at the nape of my neck. I tried to stop it, but the panic in my chest at every step they drew closer to me took my focus away.

They were going to move that trash can and find a woman with insane hair who had been spying on them.

I closed my eyes. They were almost there.

Help, please. Someone, help.

Penelope's squeal echoed through the kitchen as if she'd heard my silent plea.

"What is that?" the scary officer asked. "Get that pig out of here."

I opened my eyes and peeked around the trash can to see Penelope running circles around their feet. It took everything in me not to laugh. Penelope was a master of not being caught when she didn't want to be.

She spun one more circle before darting out of the kitchen.

Thankfully, both officers charged after her.

I didn't hesitate for even a second.

I snuck out from under the sink and glanced out the door to ensure no one was looking before darting to the back of the building and then around the other side to return to where my friend and I had been.

Penelope still had the officer's attention—running around making a racket—but when she saw I was out, she darted off toward the trucks.

The scary officer and the other one stopped and shook their heads before returning to the kitchen.

The two officers helping Katie and Renée passed me on their way back to the crime scene. Their radios went off at the same time.

"We have a report that the suspect is in row three, behind the pink and purple Peterbilt," a voice came from the mics on their shoulders.

Both officers, hands on their guns, started to run.

I knew I wouldn't be able to outrun them.

I had to use my magic. It was my only choice. Even if it hurt.

I closed my eyes and focused on the pink and purple Peterbilt—whatever that was—in row three. I pushed my magic even though it wasn't ready.

My scalp tingled, and a rush of air flooded my ears. It was working.

I pressed my eyelids closed so as not to get dizzy.

When the bellowing of the surrounding air subsided, I fell to the ground in exhaustion.

My hair draped down my shoulders in ugly gray wisps. It took everything in me to look up to see where I'd landed.

Thankfully, the pink and purple Peterbilt—a brand of semi-truck—was right in front of me. Emily, however, was nowhere to be found.

Maybe they'd gotten a false tip.

I pushed myself to a stand. I had to tell her to run before they found her.

When I turned and started toward the back of the semi, I crashed right into someone and fell backward onto my butt.

It was Emily. In the flesh.

"Are you okay?" she asked, holding out a hand to help me up.

My breath caught in my chest. What did I say? I'd planned for this moment my entire life, and now my words were frozen in my chest. Could I even speak, or had that ability drained from me?

"I—uh—"

She knelt next to me. "Are you hurt?"

The two officers appeared behind her, down the aisle of trucks. They didn't seem to see her yet.

"They're coming for you," I croaked and lifted a shaky finger. "The police. They think you killed someone. You have to hide."

5

Emily didn't hesitate. She turned and ran behind the trucks and out of sight.

I tried to get to my feet, but it was no use. I had spent all of my energy.

If only I could have followed her. I'd already broken Renée's rule about staying away from Emily. And now that I'd spoken to her, I wanted to talk more.

She was so pretty—exactly how I always imagined her. Exactly how she was in the mural. Her hair was pure white and long down her back, and her smile was like sunlight.

I sighed.

"Have you seen a blonde woman around here?" one of the officers asked as they approached me.

I shook my head. "No."

"Are you okay?" the other officer asked.

"I'm fine," I said. "Just taking a breather."

By the way I was sitting on the ground, they probably thought I was nuts. They didn't have the time to deal with me since they were looking for Emily—who had white hair, not gray like mine.

It must have taken at least fifteen to twenty minutes to muster up enough energy to get to my feet and start back toward the food pavilion.

Penelope was waiting for me, hiding under a vendor table that wasn't being used. When she saw me, she hurried over.

"You did so well." I bent down to snuggle her since I knew I didn't have the strength to pick her up. She nuzzled into me, wiggling her little piggy snout.

The weight and warmth of her body next to mine were of enormous comfort. We must have sat together on the asphalt for nearly half an hour before Nancy and Katie walked over.

Penelope hopped out of my lap, and—like magic—I felt better. Better than better. I felt refreshed.

Before I could think about what had happened too hard, Nancy and Katie started their story.

"You should have seen Katie with those officers," Nancy said. "They had no idea what they were dealing with."

The two women burst into giggles.

"Have you seen Fran and Amy?" I asked. "Or Andrea?"

"Fran and Amy are getting food to sober up," Katie said, using her fingers to air quote the words sober up.

"I saw my mom," I blurted out.

Katie and Nancy stopped laughing. Even Penelope froze next to me.

"And?" Katie asked. "Did she recognize you?"

"I don't think so," I said. "My hair was all gray and stringy. I ran right into her and told her to run because the cops were coming for her. She probably didn't have a chance to recognize me."

I'd thought about whether she'd recognize me even if my hair had been its usual white. Seeing as everyone said we looked so much alike, she was likely to.

"Did you follow her?" Nancy asked.

"I couldn't. I'd lost all my energy teleporting to her."

"Are you feeling better now?" Katie asked, pressing a hand to my forehead.

"This is going to sound crazy—"

"Oh, try us." Katie laughed.

"I think Penelope healed me," I said. "Or restored my magic."

Nancy bent down and scooped Penelope up into her arms. "Are you a magical piggy?"

Penelope wiggled her piggy snout against Nancy's cheek.

"I'll take that as a yes," Nancy said.

"Did you get to see the crime scene?" Katie asked.

"Yep." I reached for my phone in my satchel, but a scream echoed from the food pavilion before I could pull it out.

"Fran, Amy," Katie said before we all took off running toward the pavilion.

An ambulance had backed up to the kitchen door, and

the EMTs were loading a sheet-covered body into the back.

A woman with shoulder-length blonde hair was trying to claw her way out of the scary police officer's arms.

"I'd know those boots anywhere," she screamed. "That's my boyfriend."

"Your boyfriend?" A shorter woman with light brown hair screamed at the blonde. "He's my boyfriend."

"Um, excuse me?" A woman with tattoos all over her arms, wearing aviator glasses and a long brown ponytail, laughed. "Are you saying you're dating my fiancé?"

"I'm sorry, Stacie," the woman with short brown hair said. "But you know how he is. Was."

All three women stared at the ambulance's closing doors.

"But you're my best friend," Stacie said. "You knew I was going to marry him."

"I'd like to see proof," the blonde interjected. "There's no ring on your finger. And you—well—he told me about you. The sad little puppy who follows him around, begging him to take her home."

"Here's the ring." Stacie pulled a ring from her tight jeans. "Or maybe it's this one." She pulled another one from the other pocket. "I can never remember. It's why I don't wear them."

"You're engaged to two men?" the woman with light brown hair asked. "You have to be kidding me."

"I wouldn't expect you to understand," Stacie said with a shrug.

"Where are they taking him?" the blonde asked the police officer, still holding her back.

"To the morgue, ma'am." The officer let her go as the ambulance pulled away. "We'll notify—er—whoever when we know his identity for sure."

"You'll notify me," Stacie said. "I'm his fiancé."

"Like that even means anything," the blonde said.

"Give it a rest. Does your best friend know you're supposedly dating her ex-husband?"

"Oh, like you knew your best friend was supposedly dating your fiancé?"

The blonde and Stacie stared at each other with fire in their eyes.

If I were looking for actual suspects, these would be the women I'd start with. They all had motives.

I hurried over. "Hi, ladies. It's been a hard day. Why don't I buy you all a drink, and we can sit down and talk about this?"

"Who are you?" Stacie asked. "Why should we tell you anything?"

"You shouldn't," the scary police officer said.

"Are you arrestin' us?" The blonde put her hands on her hips.

"I'm not arresting anyone," the officer said. "Not yet, anyway."

"But you think one of us killed Randy?" Stacie let out a bellowing laugh. "If I were you, I'd start with that wait-ress. What's her name? Miley?"

The blonde nodded. "Yeah, definitely start with her. She hated him."

"Uh, yeah," the shorter brunette said. "She probably did it."

The police officer looked at them suspiciously. It was

the first thing they'd agreed on since they'd started arguing.

"Why does she hate him?" the officer asked.

"He never tipped her. He stayed long after closing time. And I think he hit on her a few times," the brunette said. "Before he was with me, of course."

"Psh," the blonde said with a laugh. "You think he stopped hittin' on girls the minute he turned his eyes to you?"

The brunette looked over at Stacie with wide eyes.

Stacie shrugged. "She has a point."

The brunette looked down at her feet. "No, but that doesn't mean—"

"Face it. We got played." Stacie looked over at the officer. "That waitress is probably over at the motel. She's staying there with all the other event staff. If anyone killed Randy, it was her."

The way she said his name did not make it sound like she loved him enough to marry him. But who was I to know what real love was?

The closest I'd ever been had been with a man who had utterly betrayed me.

A man who might have been dating my mother.

A man who . . . was walking toward me at that very moment.

6

Xander looked hotter than any man had any right to in leather chaps over faded blue jeans, a tight black t-shirt, and black, shoulder-length hair.

My scalp tingled, but I fought to keep my hair under control. There was no need for him to know how I was feeling.

Though, I didn't quite know how I was feeling.

Relieved he was okay.

Furious he had lied to me.

Confused about my attraction.

"Ellie, what are you doing here?" Xander asked.

"I don't have time to talk to you," I said. "I have a murder to solve."

His face went pale. "A murder?"

"Someone named Randy. You know him?"

"Heard of him," Xander said. "Maybe I can—"

I held a hand up for him to stop talking. "If you're going to offer me help, you don't need to. I have plenty of help." I motioned over to the group of women who were watching us protectively. They didn't know why I was mad at Xander, but they knew I was mad at him. And that was all they needed to know to take my side over his.

"You brought all of them to Denver to help you solve a murder?"

"Yep," I said. "Penelope's here too."

Xander's face softened at the mention of Penelope. I both wanted to slap him and hug him for that.

"I know you're probably super busy with the council stuff and all. It's not a big deal, just another crime to solve, you know?" I gave him a quick fake smile. "Gotta go."

I turned and marched over to the group of women who continued to stare Xander down, their eyes a silent warning to stay away from me.

"What does he want?" Katie asked.

"No idea," I said. "But it's awfully funny he showed up here, isn't it? Especially since he's not my guardian anymore."

"Maybe he's not here for you," Andrea said.

Katie and Nancy gasped.

"Not like that," Andrea said. "But maybe he has other things he needs to do. Or maybe this was a magical murder."

I hadn't exactly been looking for magic in anyone, but it hadn't outright jumped out at me.

I glanced back at where the women had been, but they were now gone.

"Where'd they go?"

"They skedaddled just as soon as you turned your back

on them." Nancy motioned toward the trucks. "My guess is they're all truck drivers."

"What makes you say that?" I asked.

"They all had a bright green wristband on their wrists, just like the people next to their trucks."

"That's a brilliant observation," I said. "Good eye, Nancy."

She smiled with pride.

"I guess we need to find their trucks. It'll be better to talk to them individually, anyway."

"What makes you think they'll even talk to you?" Katie asked.

I shrugged. "I don't know, but a lot is riding on this. I have to clear my mother's name."

"I hate to be the one to bring this up," Andrea said.

"Then don't," Katie said.

Andrea ignored her. "What if your mom did do it? I mean, why else would she have run from the police?"

"Because I told her to," I said.

"But if I told you to run from the police right now, would you?"

I considered this for a moment. I had no reason to run from the police. So, I likely wouldn't. Especially if a complete stranger was telling me to.

I shook my head. "I have to assume she's innocent. I'm sure she is."

"Then we need to find her before the police do," Andrea said. "Can't you do tracing spells?"

My confidence in doing tracing spells was about zero. Especially when it came to Emily. I'd tried everything I could to trace her, but even after seeing her through the mural, I'd been unable to trace her.

And today was no different.

"This is so frustrating," I said after my fifth attempt. "It's like she doesn't exist."

"I don't pretend to know how tracing spells work," Andrea said, "but are you still thinking of her as Emily Vanderwick? As your mom?"

It was as if a lightbulb had turned on inside my brain. "Of course! You're a genius. She doesn't go by Emily Vanderwick and didn't seem to recognize me as her daughter. I need to find Miley Mulroney."

"It's worth a shot," Andrea said, standing back.

Katie and Nancy had meandered off with Penelope and the other ladies to check out some trucks while we worked on the tracking spell. I suspected they were looking for the other three women who would likely be suspects in the investigation.

I concentrated on the name Miley Mulroney and what she'd been wearing when I'd last seen her. Had she smelled like lilac?

I closed my eyes and waited for the speck of magic to appear in my mind's eye. A vibration started in my scalp and wound down my spine into my chest.

A blaze of purple light nearly blinded me when I opened my eyes. I blinked back at the little globes that danced around in my vision, and as I did, the light came into focus. It was a trail leading from the food pavilion toward the trucks.

My stomach sank. Did that mean she'd been there and seen Randy dead? Or worse? Had she done it?

"Do you see something?" Andrea asked.

"Come on," I said, grabbing her by the arm and tugging her toward the purple trail. "Before it fades."

We ran down the row of trucks to where I'd run into Emily. The purple streak turned the corner where she'd run and kept going toward the event entry.

I was out of breath when we reached the front gates. "She's close," I said. "I can feel it."

Andrea looked at me with wide eyes. "Then why are we stopping?"

How was she not out of breath?

Probably because while I'd been moping around, she'd been exercising like a crazy person. Apparently, Penelope's magic didn't work on my physical fitness, just my magical fitness.

I gathered all my energy to follow the trail to the motel where the other women had told the police Emily—Miley—had gone.

Several police cars sat outside, but there didn't seem to be much action.

"Is she in one of the rooms?" Andrea asked.

I searched for the purple trail. It led past the police cars, into one of the rooms, then back out again.

"She went in and came back out," I said.

"If she got in a car, she could be anywhere."

"She didn't," I said. "The trail leads around the corner of the building."

I started slowly so as not to bring attention to myself.

The last thing I wanted to do was lead the police to my hiding mother.

When we were around the side and out of the police's view, the purple trail stopped at what looked like a flat wall. "This is where she went."

"To this wall?"

I felt around. It had to be something. "My guess is there's some magic here."

Andrea and I searched for the magic to get in but found nothing.

I sighed. "How would it just end right here? It makes no sense."

A bird let out a loud caw above us as if to answer my question.

An escape ladder leading to a doorway in the side of the building had specks of purple dancing around it.

"She went up there," I said.

"Up where?"

"Up that ladder and probably into the doorway."

Andrea looked at me like I'd been speaking gibberish. "Huh? What ladder?"

I glanced up again. "You don't see that ladder?"

She shook her head.

"Well, it's there," I said.

"You can probably only see it because of your tracking spell."

"Do you think I could climb it?" I asked.

Andrea shrugged. "You could try."

I reached up on my tip-toes and grabbed one of the ladder legs, tugging it down with all my strength. Once I could get hold of the first rung, I was able to pull it to the ground.

Andrea laughed.

"What?" I asked.

"It's just that you look hilarious. Like a mime or something."

I laughed a bit, too. "Come on. We have to get up there."

Andrea's laughter stopped. "Nope. I'm not going up some imaginary ladder."

"It's a magical ladder." I took her hand and pulled her toward it. "See, you can feel it, right?"

"Have I ever told you I'm afraid of heights? I cannot climb an invisible magical ladder to an invisible door."

"There's a platform at the top," I said. "I'll be right behind you, so if you fall, you'll fall on me."

She crossed her arms over her chest.

"Aren't you my guardian? What if my mother is a real killer and tries to kill me up there?"

Andrea looked at me with fire in her eyes. "Fine. But this better be legit."

"It'll be great," I said. "Here's the first rung. Just step up."

"I know how to climb a ladder," Andrea said.

"Maybe closing your eyes will help?"

She made her way to the top and reached for the next rung.

"You're there. Climb up onto the platform," I said.

She took a deep breath and let it out with a loud whooshing sound before she crawled on her belly across the metal grate platform.

I hurried up to the top and grabbed her hands. "Do you want to stand up?"

"I'd rather not," she said. She squeezed her eyes shut. Maybe it was a bad idea having her come up here. Getting back down would be even worse.

"I'll be quick. I'm sure once we get the door open, you'll be able to see just fine." I hurried to the door, my heart beating so loudly in my chest I could hardly hear myself think.

This was it.

This was the moment I was going to speak to my mother.

I raised a hand to knock, but my arm wouldn't function. "I can't knock."

"I know you've been through a lot of trauma," Andrea said. "But it'll be okay. Just knock."

"I don't mean like I can't because of trauma." I tried again. "I mean, I physically can't. My arm won't move." I took a step back. "Do you think you could try?"

"If you can't, why do you think I'd be able to?"

"I don't know. Maybe the protection spell is against me because she saw me and thought I was the bad guy."

My theory was flawed, of course, since I'd been the one who'd told her to run from the police.

Andrea grabbed my leg and practically climbed up on me like a baby monkey would on its mother. Her eyes were still pressed closed.

"Lead me to the door," she said.

I walked her closer to the door, careful to keep her on the side of the landing that had the railing so she wouldn't fall back down the hole for the ladder.

"It's right in front of you," I said.

She raised her arm and made a fist, but her fist didn't come into contact with the door.

"Did I do it?" she asked.

I laughed. "Did you hear or feel your hand hit a door?"

"Okay, smarty pants," she said. "If you don't want my help, I'll just go."

"No, don't go," I said. "You'll hurt yourself trying to get back down. And I need your help. Try one more time. Please?"

She raised her fist and tried to move it forward, but once again, it didn't touch the door.

"She's put some sort of protection on it," Andrea said. "A strong one."

"Magic?" I asked. "She's put magic on the door?"

"My guess is the only reason you can even see the ladder and the door is because you put a tracking spell on her."

Now that she mentioned it, the door, the ladder, and the platform all had a purple hue. "I bet you're right. But if we can't get in, then what?"

"Then we wait for her to come out," Andrea said. "After you get me back to solid ground."

7

The trip back down was much harder than the one up, but it went more smoothly once I got Andrea's feet on the ladder rungs.

"I am never doing that again," Andrea said. "I don't care if your mother is a murderer and comes out her invisible door and shoots you dead. There's no way I'm following you up an invisible ladder."

"Thank you for going," I said. "I'm sorry it scared you."

"Scared?" Andrea said. "That wasn't fear. That was terror. I don't get scared. But horror doesn't discriminate."

"Well, you did well in the face of terror."

She shook her head and walked away.

"Where are you going?"

"If we're going to have a proper stakeout, we'll need snacks. And drinks. You go hide somewhere and wait for her to come out."

She pointed to some tall grass on the other side of the alleyway.

I gave her a thumbs-up, and she hurried back toward the jamboree.

The tall grass wasn't as natural as I'd expected. I had to be careful with every step I took not to puncture the sole of my shoe with the needles littering the ground.

Once I felt sufficiently hidden, I crouched down and stared at the door I'd been unable to touch.

My stomach grumbled. How long had it been since I'd eaten? Too long. Nancy was right. I was too skinny. The muscles I'd built for years through yoga and running were now floppy and tired.

I sighed. If this didn't work out, I'd have to make sure I didn't go back into the dark cave of depression again. I'd lived this long without a mother. I could live the rest of my life without one if need be.

I peeked back up at the door when a grumbly male voice came from behind me.

"What are you doing out here, little girl?"

My body froze.

When I didn't reply, the man asked again, "What are you doing out here?"

Everything in me wanted to run, but I didn't know what this guy was capable of. I turned slowly with my palms outstretched to find a warlock giving off enough magical energy that even a non-magical human could probably see it.

"I'm not doing anything," I said.

"That's funny because it looks like you're spying on my—someone."

I narrowed my eyes. "Your who?"

"I didn't say my anyone."

"Well, I'm not spying. Who would I be spying on at the back of a building?"

"If you're not spying, then maybe you're hiding." The man stood straighter, showing off his intimidating height and muscles. He was probably in his mid-thirties with a five o'clock shadow and a tattoo of a heart with a vine wrapped around it on his upper arm. Everything about him screamed scary, but I wasn't scared.

"What are *you* doing out here?" I asked. "Maybe you're spying or hiding."

"I am not," he said, crossing his massive arms across his chest. "That's so dumb."

"If it's so dumb, then leave me alone."

"You do know I'm a warlock, right?"

"Yep," I said. "Got that."

"And I could blast your head off."

"Right, but I'm pretty sure you'd get in trouble if you did that." I smiled. "Especially since I'm next in line to be the Grand Witch of the States."

This didn't seem to faze him one bit. "I know who you are. And I know you don't belong here."

"It's only fair that I know who you are since you know who I am. I mean, if you're going to blast my head off, I might as well get to know your name."

"My name is—uh—Benderson." The way he drew out every syllable made it sound like he'd made it up on the spot.

"Benderson?" I raised my eyebrows. "Are you sure?"

"Are you teasing me for my name?"

I sighed. This was getting me nowhere. I glanced back at the building where the door and the ladder were in the same place as where I'd left them. "Look, I'm not going anywhere, so if you need to blast my head off, go ahead and do it, Benderson."

A flash of uncertainty washed over his unshaven face.

"Come on," I said. "I'll pretend you never came out here, and you can pretend I was never here, and we can both go on living our lives peacefully."

Benderson seemed to consider this but then shook his head violently. "Nope. I'm telling the police on you."

He marched out of the tall grass toward the hotel.

Crap.

If he told the police I was out here spying on the back of a hotel, they'd get suspicious and would likely come stakeout here too.

"Fine," I said, hurrying after him. "Fine, I'll leave. Just don't tell the police. It could hurt someone I—uh—care about."

Love didn't seem like the proper term, though I felt I did love Emily in my own way. If it was possible to love someone you'd never met.

"Don't come back here," he said. "This is my boundary."

"Your boundary?"

"You heard me," he yelled. "Don't come back."

As I hurried off around the corner toward the jamboree, I took one last look back at the ladder and the door, but they'd both vanished along with the magical trail.

"Why aren't you in the tall grass like I told you?" Andrea said when I came around the side of the building. She held three massive bags with savory scents wafting from whatever was inside and a drink carrier with two large sodas. "I figured we'd need our energy, and caffeine wouldn't hurt."

I rarely drank much soda, but I didn't have the heart to tell her. "Thanks." I took the drink carrier out of her hands so she could get a better grip on the bag. "But I don't think we'll be doing a stakeout tonight."

"Why not?"

"Because a massive warlock named Benderson threatened to blast my head off."

She smiled, waiting for me to finish my joke.

"I'm not kidding," I said. "It was the weirdest thing."

"But how will we talk to your mom if we don't hang out here and wait for her?"

"For now, she's safe and hidden," I said. "In the meantime, I'm going to snarf down some of the food taunting me from those bags. Then we can try to find out who the actual murderer is."

8

T he food was as delicious as it smelled. By the time I'd finished a burger, fries, and the entire soda, Katie, the gals, and Penelope, were back.

"Did you find your mom?" Nancy asked.

"Kind of," I said. "But then some big burly bully of a warlock told me to leave, or he'd turn me in to the police."

"You weren't doing anything illegal, were you?" Katie asked, her motherly voice coming through.

"We were just going to stake out the door I suspect my mother is behind."

"Did you think to knock?" Fran asked with a laugh.

"I tried," I said. "It had some sort of magical protection. And I figured since she's safe and hidden, it would be best for me to leave, so I didn't draw any police attention to the back of the building and put my mom in danger."

"What about you guys?" Andrea asked. "Did you find anything useful?"

Nancy sat forward as if waiting for this moment to arrive. "We did!"

"Let's hear it," Andrea said.

"The guy who died—Randy Howard—was the owner of one of the bigger trucking companies."

"Co-owner," Fran corrected.

I bent down and handed Penelope a French fry.

"Right co-owner with his ex-wife," Nancy said, her eyes widening with the juicy detail. "And apparently, they hate each other. Her name is Gardenia Howard, but she goes by Gar. So, Gar and that blonde from earlier—KayLynn—are best friends. Whether Gar knew KayLynn was dating her ex-husband is of much debate. Several people think Gar killed him so she could have the company all to herself."

"Tell her about the one with the tattoos—Stacie," Katie said.

Nancy squirmed in her seat. "Stacie used to work for Gar and Randy before they divorced. Gar fired her when she realized Stacie was sleeping with her husband."

"And then Randy and Stacie got engaged," Katie said.

"But Stacie didn't even know which ring was from him," I said with a laugh. "I can't imagine she cared much about being engaged to him."

"It sounds like she has a lot of men beating down her door," Fran said with a grimace.

"So, she's a truck driver?" Andrea asked.

"They all are," Nancy said. "Stacie, KayLynn, and Bridget—the brunette one."

"He had a type," I said.

"I'd venture to guess there are more women on the

list," Katie said. "But none of the others seem to be here. Or if they are, they're keeping quiet."

"Which means we have four suspects," I said.

"Well, five with your mom," Andrea pointed out. "We can't discount the fact that the other women pointed at her."

"Maybe, and I'm not saying anything bad about your mama," Fran said, "but maybe she got caught up in Randy's charms, too."

I wanted to refute her claim but couldn't. It was a distinct possibility that he'd wooed Emily, too.

"Okay, five suspects," I said. "And they all have the same motive besides one."

"Gar," Nancy said.

"Exactly," I said. "If she was going to kill him for cheating on her, why wait until now? My guess is if she's the killer, it was for money."

"Did you speak to any of the women themselves?" Andrea asked.

"They were all away from their trucks when we went by," Katie said. "But they'll have to be there for the judging tomorrow."

"And they're signed up as participants in the Jubilant Jewel Jamboree Olympics, too," Amy said.

"The Jubilant Jewel Jamboree Olympics?" I laughed. "What are the Jubilant Jewel Jamboree Olympics?"

"The truck drivers compete in several different events to see who is the Jubilant Jewel Jamboree King or Queen," Katie said.

"Do they get a prize?" I asked.

"There's a cash prize, a tiara or crown, and specialized mud flaps for their trucks."

"Sounds like a good competition," I said. "We should watch it."

The others nodded as we fell into a lull in the conversation. My brain mulled over all the information that had just been dumped on me. If these women had varying relationships with Randy and they found out he was unfaithful, they'd all have motives to kill, too.

"Ooh, I almost forgot." I pulled my phone from my satchel. "I haven't even looked at the crime scene photos."

Everyone gathered closer together so we could look at them together.

The first picture was blurry. Apparently, I'd been moving when I took it.

The second was slightly better.

"Are they all going to be like that?" Fran asked, and Amy elbowed her in the ribs.

"I was nervous and trying to hurry." I scrolled more quickly, trying to find at least one picture that wasn't blurry.

Finally, I found one. It wasn't from the best angle, but you could see most of the crime scene.

"Why is he wet?" Nancy asked.

"It looks like someone sprayed him with the dishwasher wand." Katie pointed at the sink right above his head. "See how the water sprays toward the door and his feet?"

"Could that have killed him?" Nancy asked. "I mean if the knife hadn't done the job?"

"Nah," Katie said. "They're powerful, but not like a power washer or anything."

"I think someone was trying to wash away the evidence," I said.

"That explains why there's no blood," Andrea said. "But why would they have left the knife?"

She was right. It made no sense that they went through all the trouble to clear the blood and DNA evidence but left the knife. "Are those gunshot wounds?" I pointed to where it looked like someone had shot him twice in the forearm. "Or are they tattoos? I didn't notice them when I was in there."

I passed the phone around for everyone to look at, but no one could determine whether they were real gunshot wounds or just realistic-looking gunshot tattoos.

"So he was stabbed and shot?" I asked.

"Maybe this case is too complicated for us," Amy said.

"Nah," Katie said. "Nothing's too complicated for Ellie. She's a pro."

I didn't feel like a pro, but it was nice that she felt like I was. "At what times do the judging and the Olympics start?"

Nancy looked at Katie. "They start tomorrow morning."

I glanced toward the parking lot where Mona had been all day. "I don't think we'll all fit in the van to sleep."

"I know a guy," a masculine voice said behind us. "He can get you a few nice hotel rooms."

I turned to see Xander with his hands tucked into his jeans pockets.

9

No one spoke. Everyone waited to see whether I'd take Xander up on his offer.

"Look, most local hotels are booked with all the events this weekend. I pulled some strings to get a few rooms at a magical hotel," Xander said. "When I found out you were here, I didn't want you to panic about finding a place to stay."

As much as I didn't want to take any of his favors, he had a point. We couldn't all sleep in Mona—there were too many of us—and we hadn't exactly prepared for a camping trip. Plus, a magical hotel sounded pretty cool.

"Fine," I said.

Katie cleared her throat.

"And thank you," I mumbled.

Xander nodded once. "Here's the address. When you get to the check-in warlock outside, ask for Gerald."

"Gerald, as in—" I started.

Xander interrupted. "Yes." He obviously didn't want

the others to know that Gerald was his father, though I couldn't imagine why. "Just trust me."

I almost laughed.

How could he ask us to trust him when he'd known about my mother's whereabouts but never told me? He probably knew she was here and still had said nothing about it.

"I have to go," Xander said. "But I hope the rooms are what you need to get a good night's rest."

I didn't want him to stay, but I didn't want him to leave either. Who was I kidding? I wanted to fall into his arms and return to the way we had been that night we stayed in a cave together. But too much had happened between then and now.

"Thanks," I said.

The others mumbled their thanks before he turned and walked away.

"That was awfully nice of him," Nancy said. "Maybe he's trying to make up for whatever he did wrong."

"He doesn't even seem to know he did something wrong. Or maybe he just doesn't care. Either way, yes, it was nice. But no, I'm not going to forgive him after all he's done."

"What exactly has he done?" Fran asked.

I waved a hand in the air. "Can we talk about this another time? I'm tired, and we need our rest before tomorrow's festivities." I didn't want to tell them just how badly Xander had betrayed me. Whether that was because I didn't want them to see him as a bad guy or it would make me feel worse to know they agreed with me, I didn't know. Either way, I wouldn't tell them. It didn't matter. Xander was no longer my guardian and hadn't returned to Cliff Haven since I'd seen him in the mural.

Mona was ready and raring to go. I told her the address, tickled the dash, and away we went. By the time we stopped, we could have been in California for all I knew, but with the Denver skyline out my left window, it looked like we were still in Colorado. If only I'd known this trick when I lived here, I wouldn't have had to fight the I-25 traffic all the time.

"Um, are you sure Mona took us to the right place?" Andrea asked.

I glanced out the other window and realized we were parked next to a big open field of natural grass with a no trespassing sign.

A tap on my driver's side window made me jump. I rolled it down to speak to the young warlock.

"How can I help you?"

"We're here to see Gerald."

"Ah yes," the warlock said. "We've been expecting you. Welcome to Hotel Wix."

Murmurs came from the back seat, and Penelope let out a little oink beside me.

"If you'd please take a right after the no trespassing sign, then follow the pink carpet to your rooms." He wasn't speaking to me. He was talking to Mona.

When he patted her on the door, she started moving again without my help. Apparently, she understood where to go, even if it looked like we were going to drive right into an open field.

Sure enough, the world changed around us when we drove past the no trespassing sign.

We were inside a massive structure, almost like the lobby of a grand hotel. A pink carpet led us through the lobby, past a fountain, and down a hallway.

"This can't be real, can it?" Katie asked.

Fran rubbed her eyes. "I must be dreaming."

Even being a witch, this was a lot for my brain to comprehend.

Down the hallway were six doors—each decorated differently—plus one larger door at the very end.

When we got close enough, I read the signs on each door, "Ellie and Penelope, Fran and Amy, Katie, Nancy, and Andrea. And the one at the end says, Mona."

"We each get our own rooms?" Nancy asked.

"It's a good thing," Katie said. "Nancy snores."

"I do not!" Nancy said with a laugh.

We stepped out onto the plushy pink carpet and hurried to our doors.

Mona drove the rest of the way down the hall. As if sensing her presence, the door opened, and she drove right in.

"Who wants to go first?" Nancy asked.

"Let's all go in at the same time and then come back out and compare notes," Katie said. "On three. One, two, three."

My door handle turned at the touch of my fingertips.

Gasps around me mimicked my own as I walked into the room with Penelope hot on my heels.

It was nothing short of magical.

Even though I knew it was impossible, I'd walked into a room that seemed actually to be outside. In the mountains. With a tent and an open fire pit.

The temperature was perfect. Not at all like camping in the woods, where it was always too hot or too cold. But the air was pure and fresh, as if I was outside.

Penelope followed me through the tent flap, which opened up into a room that would have been impossible to be inside that tent.

The walls were a medium gray with a large golden ornamental mirror leaning against one wall. The bed had a black headboard with the coziest-looking pillows and blankets in shades of pink and white. A large stone, wood-burning fireplace crackled in a corner.

Sometimes, magic really made me smile.

In a basket on the bed were two different yoga mats, one for me and one for Penelope.

I glanced around to find Penelope rolling around in the smaller bed next to mine with matching bedding and pillows.

Even though I hadn't brought any extra clothes to hang in the free-standing wardrobe, I still had to have a peek inside.

My heart caught in my chest when I opened the doors. Clothes, shoes, hats, scarves, and jewelry, all in my size and taste, stuffed the inside in the most organized way possible.

I couldn't wait to tell the others about it, but first, I had to check out the bathroom.

When I opened the door, another room magically changed to be much larger than the tent could accommodate and featured a sunken-in tub directly in the center of the room. Steam and bubbles called to me. A shower with multiple shower heads and a bench stood on one wall, and on the other was a door that probably led to the toilet. A sink and vanity area stood close to the entry door, and even though the room was very steamy, the mirror was steam-free.

I let out a squeal of joy. "How cool is this, Penelope?"

Penelope let out a squeal of her own.

"We should go see what the others' rooms look like."

She and I met at the door leading to the hallway, but no matter how hard I tried, it wouldn't open back up.

My dream room had turned into my prison.

I tried the handle again, but it still wouldn't budge.

Though I knew it wouldn't work since this was a magical room, I tried to use my magic to teleport outside the room into the hall or even back to the jamboree, but everything I tried failed miserably.

"Penelope, my magic is useless here," I said.

As if sensing the worry in my voice, Penelope hurried to my side and wiggled her nose on my leg.

"I hope everyone else is okay," I said, trying my cell phone and finding it dead. "What if they're all stuck too? The only ones who have each other are Fran, Amy, and you and me."

There were no outlets to plug in a charger, just that stupid beautiful fireplace and the mock outdoors.

As tears started welling up in my eyes, a phone rang inside the tent.

I rushed in and found a rotary-style phone like one I'd seen in an antique store on the nightstand.

The ring was haunting. "Do I answer it?"

Penelope let out a low grumble.

"My thoughts exactly," I said. "But it's probably the only way we'll get out of here."

I sucked in a breath and marched over to the phone. I needed to demonstrate that I wasn't afraid, especially since there could easily be cameras or magical ways of watching my every move.

Just the thought creeped me out.

The ivory phone handle was cold, despite the room's warmth. The circular metal ear and mouthpieces were also cold as I put them up to my face. "Hello?"

"Hello, Ellie," a man's voice came through the receiver. "This is Gerald Wix. I'd like to welcome you to Hotel Wix."

"Yes, I believe we've met before. Thank you for Mona. Now, why have you locked me in my room?"

"I thought you'd take a bit more time to enjoy the comforts of the room specifically tailored to your heart."

"It's a beautiful room, but when I'm not allowed to leave, it feels more like a beautiful prison."

He let out a hearty laugh. He didn't sound like a creep or a jerk. He sounded like a sweet, warm, fatherly type. "I assure you. I do not mean it to be a prison. I simply had a few things I wanted to speak with you about before you rejoined your friends."

"Are they okay? Are they trapped in their rooms, too?"

"Of course not," he said. "They're enjoying a home-cooked meal in your group's private dining room."

"What do you want to speak with me about?" I asked.

"I want you to leave Colorado," he said. "What's happening here is none of your concern."

"If you wanted me to leave, why did you offer me a place to stay?"

"It was the only way I'd have the chance to speak with you," he said. "You understand?"

"The only thing I understand is that you are holding us captive here. Which is illegal both in non-magical and magical law books. Does Xander know about this?"

"Xander only wanted to help," Gerald said, not answering my question.

"I'm not leaving," I said. "I need to help clear my mother's name. Yes, I know she's here. I saw her."

"I, too, knew she was here, as does Xander," he said. "Does Xander know you know?"

"Does it matter?"

He hesitated before answering. "I suppose not."

"You can't make me leave," I said. "You can try to use magic to keep me here, but Renée will come looking for me eventually, and when she finds me, you'll be in a world of hurt."

"Whoa, whoa, whoa," he said. "Let's take a breath. I am not holding you captive, nor will I use any sort of force —magical or otherwise—to make you leave the state. I am simply asking you to leave well enough alone for your mother's sake. You will ruin everything if you get too close."

A thought crossed my mind, and my chest tightened. "Did you have something to do with her disappearance? Have you been holding her captive? Is she captive in the back of that hotel, and that thug was there on your account to scare me away?"

"Thug?" He laughed again. "Your idea of a thug differs greatly from mine."

"Answer my questions," I said.

"I don't have to answer anything."

"Then let me go," I said. "My friends and I will stay somewhere else tonight. Heck, we'll stay in Mona if necessary."

"Don't say I didn't warn you," he said before the line went dead.

The door handle opened easily when I returned. I scooped up Penelope and my satchel and hurried out the door.

Coming down the hallway toward me were all of my friends.

"Come on, we're leaving," I said.

"Why?" Nancy asked with a shocked look on her face.

"I was just trapped in there by Xander's father," I said. "He basically threatened me and told me to leave Colorado. And he may be holding my mother captive."

"Xander's father?" Andrea asked, wide-eyed. "Did you see him?"

"He called me on the phone," I said.

"Do we have to leave? My room is so nice," Nancy whined.

"Mine is, too," I said, then turned toward the garage door at the end of the hall. "Mona, come on."

The door opened, and Mona slowly drove toward me as if she was pouting like all my friends.

"Xander's father—Gerald Wix—locked you in your room?" Andrea asked, her voice slightly panicked. "Did he say where he was?"

"No, but he told me I need to leave the state." I opened Mona's sliding door and motioned for everyone to get in.

"I'll get us a nice hotel room tonight," I said. "A non-magical hotel room."

"Why does he want you to leave the state?" Andrea asked as we drove out of the hotel and back onto the street. The building that had been there shimmered and disappeared, leaving a wide-open space of tall grass.

"Magic is so cool," Amy said.

I wanted to shake them all. Had Gerald put them under some sort of spell? Was that even possible?

"He said I'm going to make things worse for Emily," I said. "But I don't trust him."

"Nor should you," Andrea said. "He's not a good man. If you had told me he was the hotel's owner, I never would have allowed us to stay there."

So that's why Xander didn't want me to say Gerald was his father.

"What has he done?" I asked.

I drove myself, not letting Mona take control. Up I-25 was a hotel I'd always seen as impossibly expensive, but now—with the help of my wealthy grandmother's inheritance—I would make the impossible possible.

"I can't divulge that," Andrea said. "But I'm not letting you out of my sight."

I didn't object. If she'd been in the room with me, she

might have been able to help me get out. Or talked to Gerald. Or something.

We pulled up to the hotel and let a non-magical human valet park Mona. Before I got out, I whispered, "No funny business. He's just going to park you. I'll be back soon."

I could almost hear her groan.

Even the valet looked around at the funny sound.

I smiled. If only he knew.

"Come on, wipe those grumpy expressions off your faces. This is the fanciest hotel in Denver. It's going to be great."

My friends stared at me as if I was still crazy for taking them from their magical, happy places. The only one who didn't look like she was about to overthrow my authority was Andrea.

"Do you think they've been put under some sort of spell?" I whispered to her as we followed the others through the sliding doors.

"I can't tell," Andrea said. "I mean, those rooms were pretty nice, the food was delicious, and it sucks we have to stay at a non-magical hotel. But security was a serious issue. When I get my hands on Gerald, he'll have another thing coming."

"I'm okay," I said. "I don't think he's going to do anything. He just said I'm going to mess everything up. But how? How could I possibly mess anything up?"

"Something is going on," Andrea said. "When you see Xander next, you need to have a heart-to-heart and get to the bottom of it."

"He doesn't even know that I know about him knowing about my mom."

"Wait, say that again slower," Andrea said.

"I'm still mad and don't want to discuss anything with him," I said.

She didn't respond before we were at the check-in desk.

"How can I help you lovely ladies tonight?" The man behind the desk was tall and lanky, with a crispy mustache and matching hair, almost like he gelled them both at the same time.

"We'd like six rooms, please," I said.

"Five," Andrea said. "I'm staying with you and Penelope. There's no way I'm letting you out of my sight again."

"Fine," I said. "Five rooms."

"Would you like our cheaper rooms or something more luxurious?"

"What's your most luxurious?" I asked.

"Now, don't do that just because we had to leave that other place," Katie said. "You don't need to be spending all your money on us."

The man's eyebrows raised toward his hairline at the mention of us leaving another hotel, but he said nothing.

"I'm happy to," I said. "I don't have much to spend it on at home."

"The penthouse has seven rooms on two floors, with an open kitchen and living space and a large balcony."

"We'll take that one," I said.

The penthouse wasn't as perfect as the room at Hotel Wix. The floor was white marble, and everything was more pristine than cozy. But it still widened my friends' eyes when we walked in.

As they explored the bedrooms, whatever spell or disappointment they'd had from the last place seemed to wear off, leaving them content with our current situation.

"I know all of you already ate," I said. "But I'm starving. Penelope, do you want to join me to go search for some food?"

"I'm coming with you," Andrea said.

"I'll be fine," I said. "I've been in downtown Denver hundreds of times in my life."

"I don't care," Andrea said. "Things are different now. You didn't know then that you were next in line to be the Grand Witch of the States."

"But I still was next in line."

She gave me a scathing look. "Also, the magical world didn't know you existed."

"Fine, you can come."

Penelope waited by the elevator door as we shouted our goodbyes up the stairs to the others.

"We'll be back in no time," I said. "Maybe you could find a movie for us to watch."

"On it!" Nancy said, hurrying back down the stairs.

I pushed the button for the elevator, and the doors chimed open as if the lift had been waiting for us.

"After you," Andrea said.

I'd been craving my favorite pho restaurant for months since I'd been in Iowa. Not that Iowa didn't have good food, it did. But the more specialized places like sushi and pho were less prevalent.

"Here we are," I said.

"This is where you want to eat?" Andrea said with a look of disgust.

"It's the best in the city," I said. "I love hole-in-the-wall joints."

"Ellie!" Juliette—the restaurant owner—shouted from behind the counter. "I thought you died! And Penelope! It's so good to see the two of you!"

She hurried out and wrapped her arms around my neck, pulling me down since she was much shorter than me.

"We had to move pretty abruptly," I said with a laugh. I'd never considered anyone would have missed us. No one usually did. But I suppose I'd been visiting this restaurant for years.

"Do you want your usual?" she asked. "And an extra bowl for your friend?"

"Oh no, I'm not hungry," Andrea said.

"Yes, please," I said. "That would be wonderful."

She hurried into the back to dish up a bowl of broth, meat, veggies, and extra helpings of yummy noodles while we sat in the booth by the window.

The restaurant was empty besides Juliette, which was usual when Penelope and I visited. I often wanted to ask her how she kept her business open with so few customers, but I didn't want to be rude.

"This is your favorite place, huh?" Andrea asked, still looking around like the place was rat-infested or something.

"Yes," I said. "And I'd appreciate it if you wouldn't ruin it for me."

"I don't want to ruin it for you, but have you noticed this place is magical?"

"I—" I glanced around with a different focus, and sure enough, the magic appeared at the edge of my vision.

"There's a reason you're attracted to it," Andrea said.

"But the food—"

"I'm sure the food is delicious," Andrea said. "But you didn't come in here the first time for the food. Something else brought you to this part of town."

I tried to think back to the first time Penelope and I had visited. Then it hit me: Penelope hadn't been with me the first time I visited. In fact, it was the next day that I found Penelope. Just down the street from here.

Could I have been attracted to this place because it was my window to get Penelope?

I glanced down at my best friend in the whole world. When she looked up at me, I could have sworn she winked.

"But—how—why—"

"Food for you," Juliette said, placing a bowl of soup and an extra plate of noodles in front of me. "I'll be right back with Penelope's."

Penelope oinked like normal.

"But Juliette isn't a witch," I said when Juliette returned to the kitchen. "And this is her restaurant."

"You're right. She's not a witch," Andrea said. "Which makes this all the more interesting, don't you think?"

I was starting to hate all the moments when magic caught me off guard. Was I ever going to figure it all out, or did this happen to all witches and warlocks?

The aroma of the soup hit my nose, and my stomach growled.

At least I knew one thing for sure: this soup would be the best meal I'd had in months.

Penelope and I devoured our food in record time, and Juliette even brought us extra plates of noodles before we paid the bill and made our way back out to the bustling streets of downtown Denver.

"Do you think someone put magic on this place so it would be kept only for me?" I felt stupid even thinking that, but Andrea smiled.

"That's exactly what I think," she said. "I didn't tell you when we walked up, but I couldn't see the door. Even when we were inside, the place looked like a dirty alley with a broken picnic table, and your food smelled like rotting produce."

My mouth fell open. "You have to be kidding."

She shook her head. "And that woman you were talking to? She has no idea."

"But then, how does she keep the store open? And does she really think I'm her only customer? If so, how did she believe her business was working when I hadn't been here for months?"

"All good questions," Andrea said. "And none that I can answer. But I think the real question should be, who set this up? Especially since no one in the magical world knew you existed."

Only one person came to mind—Gerald.

Anger flooded through me. "Why would someone go through all the trouble to set something like this up for me but let me be tossed around from foster home to foster home my entire childhood?"

Andrea didn't reply. Penelope let out an angry oink on my behalf. At least she was on my side.

"Come on, we better get back to watch the movie, or they'll start without us," I said, marching off toward the hotel.

"Before we go back," Andrea said. "There's someone I need you to speak with."

I whipped around to find Xander standing next to Andrea as if he'd appeared out of thin air.

"I don't want to speak to him," I said through gritted teeth. "I already told you that."

"You don't want to speak with me? Why?" Xander looked genuinely confused.

My temper got the best of me, and words started

spewing out of my mouth. The thing was, I didn't want to stop them anymore. I was tired of holding everything in.

"Maybe because your father trapped me in his stupid hotel and convinced all my friends that they were better off there. Maybe because someone has been toying with me my entire life, acting like they were helping when they were just controlling. Maybe because I struggled for years to fit in somewhere when I didn't know a magical community existed." I took a breath, tears welling in my eyes. "Or maybe it's because I know all about your relationship with my mother."

13

Xander looked genuinely concerned about all the points I was making.

Tears streamed down my face now, and Penelope nuzzled into my leg. I picked her up and held her tightly to my chest.

"It sounds like the two of you have a lot to discuss," Andrea said. "I'm going back to the hotel. I'll let the others know you won't make it for the movie. Xander, you can protect her, right?"

I didn't want protection. Didn't want to talk to Xander. But now it was all out there, and there was no other option.

"I can," Xander said.

Andrea nodded and walked away.

"Where do you want to go to talk?" I asked.

"Would you like some coffee?" He shifted his weight from one foot to the other like a middle school boy asking a girl to his first dance.

"Coffee is fine."

He led Penelope and me to the nearest coffee shop. He ordered me a latte, Penelope a whipped cream cup, and him a black coffee before bringing them to the booth I'd chosen in the back corner of the room.

I took a sip and closed my eyes. I needed to calm down and listen to what he had to say. "I'd like you to explain everything to me. All of it. No detail is too small."

Xander took a sip of his coffee. "First, I need you to tell me about the hotel. Did you speak to my father? Was he there?"

"He called me on the phone," I said. "He told me to leave Colorado, or I would mess everything up."

"Interesting," Xander said.

"Nope, no sir," I said. "You will not just say interesting and then not explain what is going on. Why is that interesting? Why did he do that? Did you know he was going to do that?"

"I assure you. I had no idea. I thought I could trust him, but I was mistaken," Xander said. "Let's start from the beginning, shall we?"

I almost shouted—*Yes! That's exactly where we should start!*—but instead, I just nodded.

"Your mother made a choice when she found out she was pregnant with you to protect you at whatever cost," Xander said.

My heart was beating so fast I thought I might pass out. This was the information I'd been waiting for my entire life, but now I didn't know if I was ready to hear what he had to say.

I had no choice. I needed to know, even if it wasn't the story I wanted to hear.

"Emily had someone—my father—remove her memories the moment after she left you at the fire station."

"Remove her memories? Like of everything? Why?"

"She knew she'd be putting you in danger if someone were to find out she had a child."

"But Harriet remembers," I said. "Couldn't she have been targeted?"

"She was a child. Even my father—the *businessman* he is—wouldn't touch a child's memory."

"Emily didn't remember me? That's why she never came for me? That's why she never went back to Cliff Haven?"

Xander nodded. "She was in the hospital a while with amnesia, but eventually—when the doctors realized her memories weren't coming back—a charity helped her get back on her feet. She got a job at the diner and has been living as Miley ever since."

"Was the danger from Monroe?"

"Yes," Xander said.

"Then why can't your father take the spell back now? Monroe is dead. He's not a threat anymore."

"She has a life now," Xander said. "A non-magical life. If we reintroduced her old memories, it could overwhelm her and put her into a coma."

"What about all the people who remember her? Why didn't any of them go looking for her?"

"My father hid her for a long time," Xander said. "And I suspect he altered their minds, too. Something that would distract them if they were to look too hard for her."

"But you knew where she was," I said. "I saw you together at the diner."

Xander's eyes widened. "You saw us together?"

"Are you dating her?" I asked, my voice only coming out as a whisper.

Xander didn't reply right away, and my chest felt like it might implode.

Finally, he said, "No. We're not dating."

"Then why didn't you tell me you found her? You promised."

"I was so excited when I found her. It was only about a month after I formally met you. But when I talked to her, she wasn't Emily. Not only because she'd changed her name, but she remembered nothing. I tried to be as sly as I could when bringing things up, but every time I did, she genuinely didn't know what I was talking about. Once I asked her if she ever traveled anywhere, and she said she'd never been outside of Colorado."

"So she doesn't remember Esme or Jake or anything?"

Xander shook his head. "As far as I can tell, she remembers nothing from her life before she left that fire station."

"You still could have told me," I said.

"I didn't know what to tell you. She wasn't your mother. And my father gave me the same warning as he's given you. To leave her alone or else things could go badly."

I slammed my fist on the table, making Xander's coffee splash from his mug, and Penelope's head shot up from her cup. Even her cute little whipped cream mustache didn't make me smile.

"This is unacceptable," I said. "He needs to restore her memories. Now."

Xander didn't say anything for a long while. I was ready to stand up and walk out the door when he reached out and grabbed my hands.

Warm pulses of electricity shot up my arms when his fingertips touched my hands.

"I want you to have your mother," Xander said. "More than anything. But we have to be careful. If you talk like you're her daughter, and she gets flashes of her memory, we could lose her all together."

"We?" I asked. "What do you mean, we?"

"I've developed a great fondness for her," Xander said. "She's almost like an older sister to me. We're good friends."

My eyes filled with tears, but I didn't want to let go of his hands to wipe them away. "I want to be her friend. Even if she never knows she's my mother. I want her in my life."

"Do you think you can handle that kind of boundary?"

"I think so."

He sighed. "I suppose now that you understand the dangers of bringing the past to light, you aren't as much of a threat as before. But first, I need you to tell me more about Hotel Wix."

ander walked Penelope and me back to the hotel, all the way to the elevator doors in the lobby.

"I can make it upstairs just fine," I said. "But thanks for watching out for me."

"I've been looking for my father for months, but once I find him, we'll talk to him about reversing the spell. Maybe it's not what I think. Maybe she had him create a backdoor, so to speak, for a time just like this." He cupped a hand to the side of my face. "I'm so sorry I didn't tell you when I found her. Do you know how hard it was to lie to you?"

"Not hard enough, apparently," I said, turning away from him to push the elevator button. "I'll work on finding the actual killer. Let me know if you hear from your dad."

The elevator doors opened, and Penelope and I stepped in.

"Bye, Ellie."

"Bye."

When the doors closed, I leaned against the mirrored wall and let the tears fall down my face.

My mother might never know me.

Ever.

When the doors slid open to a dark penthouse, I was silently thankful that the others had gone to bed. I didn't need them worrying about me and my mental state.

I climbed into the twin-sized bed in the room that was obviously made for children but was the only room with two beds. Andrea sat in her bed, holding her e-reader tablet. "Everything okay with Xander?"

"Yep," I said. "Goodnight."

I closed my eyes and drifted off to sleep within seconds.

"Are you ready for the Jubilant Jewel Jamboree Olympics to begin?" a voice boomed from the surrounding speakers.

Katie and the others didn't ask about my night, which meant Andrea probably hadn't told them I'd been with Xander. We stood on the sidelines of a large open concrete patch just inside the front gates of the jamboree, where ten women had lined up, ready to tackle the obstacles in front of them.

The three women I most wanted to see—and talk to—were disbursed among the group, throwing each other nasty looks now and then.

"That's Gar," Nancy said, pointing to the woman with

the microphone telling everyone what the rules and such were for the events. "She's Randy's ex-wife."

"Right," I said. "And the short brunette is Bridget, who used to be best friends with Stacie until Stacie realized Bridget was dating her fiancé."

"Yes," Katie said. "And KayLynn is the blonde who is best friends with Gar, though I'm not sure if Gar knows that KayLynn and Randy were together."

"Stacie used to work for Gar's company," Nancy continued. "But Gar fired her when she found Stacie and Randy together."

My head spun. That was a lot of information to keep in my mind. But basically, they all had motives to kill him . . . and possibly each other.

"On your mark, get set, go!" Gar yelled into the mic.

Stacie was in the lead, her tattoos even more visible today, with a cleavage-baring tank top and teeny tiny cutoff jean shorts. This woman might have had zero flesh without a tattoo besides the skin on her face.

As Stacie flipped the massive semi tire down the cement, it was apparent she had the physical advantage in the competition.

"And look what we have here. The treacherous cheating floozy is in the lead," Gar deadpanned.

The crowd laughed.

Stacie shot her a glare that almost looked like a warning. But Gar didn't seem to mind.

"Why isn't KayLynn even trying?" Katie asked.

KayLynn stood at the starting line with her hands on her hips. She wore a pair of black leggings and an oversized t-shirt with a semi-truck on the front.

"Maybe this just isn't her event," Nancy said. "I bet she'll join in on one of the others."

"Gar did say that it's a cumulative score throughout all the events," I said.

"Oh wow, did you see that, folks? Bridget the widget just fell on her lying, cheating buttooshka." Gar laughed so loudly into the mic the speaker screeched.

The crowd shouted, each person covering their ears from the horrible sound.

"Okay, moving on, Stacie wins. Big shocker. If you could clear the rest of the tires off the course with those manly muscles, I'd appreciate it. Thanks." Gar didn't make eye contact with Stacie as she moved to a different section of the course.

KayLynn followed closely behind her.

"This next event will test the truck drivers' smarts." Gar covered her mouth with her hand as if telling a secret. "Don't tell her I said this, but I'm pretty sure Stacie's not winning this one."

Several people in the crowd burst out laughing again. It was obvious who did and didn't like Stacie. Or maybe people just thought Gar was playing around.

If they'd seen the look on Stacie's face, they'd have known it wasn't a joke to her. In fact, she looked mad enough to kill.

"We're going to give each of the truckers a map of the event. They will have to navigate the course on their big wheel tricycles, find the clues, and get back here with the last clue before anyone else."

This seemed like a mixture of smarts and athleticism,

but maybe the speed didn't count as much as knowing how to solve the clues.

KayLynn was practically jumping up and down for joy when she mounted her adult-sized big wheel tricycle and waited for the sign to rip open the first clue.

Gar lifted the microphone to her lips. "Are you ready?"

The ten women nodded.

"Then go!"

Envelopes tearing was the only sound for a few seconds. But when KayLynn took off on her big wheel, the crowd erupted and chased after her.

Several shouted for her to tell them the clue.

"No helping," Gar reminded the crowd. "She can tell you what she's looking for, but you can't do the work for her."

"I'm not telling them anyhow," KayLynn said.

The crowd booed and turned their attention to Bridget, who was next to head out.

Stacie seemed to be struggling to read her note.

"Is this a joke?" Stacie finally asked when the rest of the truckers had pedaled off. "Or are you purposely trying to sabotage me?"

15

Gar didn't even acknowledge Stacie as Stacie continued to struggle with the note.

"Can someone help me?" Stacie asked. "This is gibberish."

Finally, Gar turned to look at her. "It's not my fault if you can't read."

Stacie's face turned a nasty shade of red before she charged at Gar.

When Stacie was about ten feet away, Gar pulled a knife from her pocket and lunged at Stacie.

What was left of the crowd—the ones who hadn't gone after the truckers on trikes—gasped.

Stacie tried to stop but, in her haste, tripped over her own two feet and fell into a wailing heap on the concrete.

"Help," Stacie cried. "My ankle is broken, and that psycho is going to kill me like she killed her ex-husband."

Another gasp came from the crowd.

Katie pushed me forward. "Now is your chance to talk to her. Go fix her ankle."

"Does anyone know first aid?" Gar mumbled, returning the knife to her pocket.

"I do." I hurried onto the course and bent down next to Stacie.

By the angle of her foot, the ankle was broken.

"Do you mind if I feel for a pulse?" I asked. "Just to make sure your foot still has blood flow?"

"Whatever you need to do," Stacie said through gritted teeth. Tears streamed down her face.

I gently placed three fingers on her ankle. She likely didn't know that if I wanted to check a pulse for her foot, I'd have to get to the top of her foot, which was currently covered by tennis shoes.

But I wasn't actually checking for a pulse. My touch was the only way I could heal her.

The moment my skin contacted hers, pain shot up my arm—her pain. But I didn't wince or pull back. I'd been ready for it.

Holding my hand on her ankle, I could feel the bones clicking back into place.

And as the pain subsided, another emotion surfaced.

Fear.

I tried to lean into the feeling but couldn't get past the overwhelming sense of fear.

When I glanced up at Stacie, I expected her to be watching me. Instead, her eyes were on Gar.

"I don't think it's broken," I said, trying to draw her attention back to me to see if her emotions had changed.

Sure enough, they went from fear to relief when she looked at me. "It's not? I could have sworn I felt it crack."

"Probably just the ankle bone scraping on the

concrete," I said, making up something completely ridiculous to explain away the magic I'd just performed. "Can you move it?"

She twisted her foot. "It's still sore, I think. But it's feeling better. Thank you so much."

I held my hands up. "I didn't do anything. It was probably a shock to your system. We should ice it, though."

She nodded. "I didn't want to win this stupid competition, anyway."

Gar glared at her and reached for her pocket.

She was awfully trigger-happy with that knife. Maybe that was her weapon of choice. And if so, maybe she'd been the one to kill her ex.

Stacie and I walked to the food pavilion while Katie and the others stayed back to watch the end of the race.

"Why don't you sit down here?" I said, helping Stacie into a chair. "I'll get some ice."

"Thank you," Stacie said. "You really don't have to do that."

"It's okay. I don't mind." Part of me felt guilty that I had ulterior motives for helping, but this might be my only chance to talk to her alone.

"Can I please have a bag of ice?" I asked the woman bent down beneath the counter. She seemed to be looking for something, but she jolted to a stand when she heard my voice.

My knees went weak. It was Emily.

"A bag of ice, you said?"

She was stunning. Her white hair practically sparkled even though the light was dim, but for the life of me, I couldn't see any magic surrounding her. Maybe she had given up her magic when she'd given up her memories.

"Are you okay?" she asked, waving a hand in front of my face.

"Oh." I shook my head. "Sorry. I'm fine. Just a bag of ice if you have one."

"You're the woman who told me to run yesterday, aren't you?" She glanced at my hair. "I like the new hair color."

"Yeah," I said, pushing my blonde braid over my shoulder.

"How did you know the police were after me? Or where I was?"

"Someone spotted you and called it in over the radio. I heard it and wanted to warn you."

She nodded slowly. That didn't really answer her question, but I couldn't tell her the truth. I didn't want to cause her brain any permanent damage.

"Well, thank you," she said. "But I went and spoke with the police last night. I didn't want to run. Plus, I have a job to do. Bills, you know?"

She turned and started filling a bag with ice.

"I guess that means the police don't think you killed Randy," I said, hope growing in my chest.

"They probably still think I did," she said. "But they have no proof, and they won't get any either. I'm innocent."

She walked back up to the counter and handed me the bag of ice.

"How much do I owe you?" I asked.

"It's ice, sweetheart," she said with a warm laugh.

"You don't owe me anything. But come back and get some of my famous pancakes when you have a chance. They have crispy edges to die for."

I froze. I loved crispy-edged pancakes. They were the most delicious things in the entire world. And Jake—the Cliff Haven Police Chief and the man I once thought was my father—loved them too. Maybe because she used to make them for him.

"Do you have any kids?" she asked me. "I mean, you're young, so you might not, but I thought I'd ask. Sorry if that's too personal."

"Uh—no—it's not," I said. "And, no, I don't have any kids."

"That's too bad," she said. "I have a daughter."

My heart did a little flip-flop. "You do?"

"Yep," she said, pride flowing through her voice. "I haven't seen her in a while, but I'm sure she's out there doing all the things."

Was she talking about me? Did she remember me, after all?

"That's great," I said, clearing my throat. "Do you know her name?"

She laughed. "Of course I do. I named her."

I let out a nervous laugh. "Right. That was a stupid question."

"No, no, no," she said. "There's no such thing as stupid questions."

I wanted to ask more about her daughter, to know what else she knew. Obviously, she didn't know I was her daughter, but maybe she had an inkling because we looked so much alike.

"If I see her, I'll introduce you," Emily said. "She's about this tall, has long, curly white hair, and talks a mile a minute."

Confusion marred my thoughts. When she'd talked about her daughter's height, she'd set her hand right below her collarbone.

"You mean your daughter is here?"

"Somewhere," Emily said. "She's not supposed to leave the event. She's only nine, though she acts like she's an adult. Her name's Eloise."

My head was as light as a helium balloon. I felt like I might pass out. Emily had a daughter—another daughter. I had a sister. A real sister.

Did Xander know?

Why didn't he tell me?

My hand was so cold.

I glanced down to see the ice melting in the bag.

"I—uh—have to get this to Stacie," I said. "Have a g-good day."

She gave me a strange look. "You too. Come back for those pancakes, okay?"

Was that the real reason Xander couldn't let her old memories and her new ones come into focus? Because she'd go from having one daughter to two? Maybe having a husband but still being in love with whoever my father was? She'd named her daughter Eloise. It was so close to Ellie. And she had the signature Vanderwick white hair. Did she have magic? Did her hair change too?

"Thanks for the ice," Stacie said, taking the bag from my hand when I didn't offer it to her.

"No problem," I said, sinking into the seat across from her.

"Did I see you over there talking to Miley Mulroney?"

"Mm-hmm," I said.

"I'm surprised the cops let her go," Stacie said. "It's obvious she's the one who killed Randy."

"Why do you say that?"

"He died in her food stall, for one."

I glanced up. The stall where he'd died was still cordoned off with police tape. "Then why is she in that one?"

"I'm sure they had an opening. And everyone loves her pancakes. They're crazy addictive. But I'd be careful eating anything from her. That's probably how she did it, with poison in his pancakes. That would make a good cozy mystery title. Do you read?"

"Not really," I said.

"Cozy mysteries have all these funny, punny titles. Poison in his pancakes. I should write that book."

"Do you write?" I asked.

"Not really," she replied with a wink.

"Do you think someone might have been setting it up to look like Em—Miley—killed him?"

Stacie looked at her ankle and shrugged. "Who knows? But that seems a bit far-fetched, right? Like someone would kill him and then take him to her stall just to set her up to look like the murderer. The police would have to have more evidence than that to arrest her."

"But they didn't arrest her," I said.

"They were going to," Stacie said. "But then she turned herself in."

"And they released her. Doesn't that show that they didn't have enough evidence to charge her with anything?"

Stacie shrugged. "I'm not a cop, so I don't know."

I sighed. "Let's say, hypothetically speaking, it wasn't Miley. Who else would want Randy dead?"

"Gar, for sure," she said almost too quickly.

"Why do you say that?"

"She had the most to gain from his death."

"The company?"

"And all his life insurance and stuff," Stacie said. "We fought about it all the time. He added Gar back onto the documents after they divorced and refused to change his paperwork until he married someone else."

"But the two of you were engaged, right? Had you set a date?"

"We hadn't nailed anything down yet."

"Did I hear that you might have been engaged to someone else too?"

Stacie laughed. "Not exactly. Not at the same time. I'm sure the ring thing throws everyone off. I have a couple of extra rings. They're from old fiancés. Everyone knows you get to keep the ring if you break up. So, I still have them."

"Why?"

"They're my retirement plan. Especially now that my future husband is dead." Her voice did not have any inflection of sadness.

"I hate to ask this, but what kind of relationship did the two of you have?"

"Why? Because I don't sound like I care?"

I shrugged.

"Look, we had an agreement. He and I worked well together. In all honesty, I knew he had women on the side, and he knew I had men on the side. But whenever we were in the same town, it was only the two of us. I've never been the gushy emotional type, but he loved that about me."

"Can you tell me more about him and the other two?"

"Bridget and KayLynn? Well, Bridget is my best friend." She air-quoted the words best friend. "She didn't think I knew they were sleeping together. But I knew. Randy and I didn't have secrets from one another. He didn't love her—he just needed a side piece. He didn't like to sleep in a bed alone. So, when Bridget was around, and no one else was, she was his companion of choice."

"And KayLynn?"

"She's a nothing, no-good, gold digger," Stacie said. "She thought she was going to get the ring. When she found out I did, I thought she'd come out of her skin. But that didn't stop her from chasing him like a cat chases a mouse."

"Do you think either of them could have killed him?"

"No," she said, her voice definitive. "They're too wimpy to kill anyone. KayLynn didn't even try to compete in the tire flip."

"I'm sure you've talked to the police and given them your alibi," I said. "But do you mind telling me too?"

She narrowed her eyes at me. "Why are you asking me all this?"

"I'm just curious," I said. "I like true crime, maybe a little too much."

"Podcasts or tv shows?"

My insides tightened. If she were to quiz me on either, I'd have no way of fudging my way through it. I didn't watch much TV other than movies with Penelope, and I didn't listen to podcasts.

"TV," I finally said.

"Oh. I'm more of a podcast girl. In the truck, you know?"

Right. I should have thought of that. She probably didn't watch much TV either.

"Have any good recommendations? Maybe I'll try a podcast on my way home."

"*My Favorite Murder* is my absolute favorite one. The hosts are amazing, and their stories are so well done."

"So, if they were doing a show about this murder, who would they think did it?"

She contemplated this for a few moments. "Gar. Definitely Gar."

17

When I returned to the Olympics, KayLynn had just crossed the finish line and was doing a celebratory dance.

The crowd cheered.

"How'd it go with Stacie?" Katie asked when I came back to stand by her.

"Fine," I said. "Her ankle is okay, but I got her ice, anyway."

I almost told her about Emily and Eloise, but if I told her that Emily was only yards away, she'd march right over there and ruin everything. The only person I could talk to about it was Xander, and I didn't know where Xander was at the present moment. Hopefully, out finding his dad.

"She thinks Gar is to blame for the murder and that she set it up to make it look like Emily did it."

"Why would Gar try to frame Emily?"

"No clue," I said. "I should have asked her that."

"Look at this." Katie held up a piece of paper. "This is the note that Gar gave Stacie for the first clue."

I held the note up and tried to make sense of the message. The words were all in English, but they weren't strung together in sentences that made any sense. "She sabotaged her."

"That's what it looks like."

"Which could mean she's only pointing the finger at Gar because she wants revenge."

"That's entirely possible," Katie said. "But did you see how quickly Gar pulled that knife out of her pocket? And wasn't there a knife sticking out of Randy's chest?"

I nodded. "I noticed the knife skills, too."

"We need to talk to Gar," Katie said. "She probably has a whole different perspective on the situation."

"I bet they all do. The problem is getting them to talk to us individually without rousing suspicion."

"They're all going to be separated this afternoon when the truck judging happens," Katie said. "I think that'll be our chance."

We watched as three other women crossed the finish line before Bridget. Stacie had hobbled over to cheer Bridget on. I couldn't imagine how hard it would be to find out my best friend was sleeping with my fiancé. Stacie put on a good face, but when Bridget had been outed, Stacie had looked genuinely surprised.

"For the last event," Gar said into the microphone. "We're going to have a test of safety. As you can see, ten trucks are parked in a line at the front of the event. Each of them has various things wrong with them. Truck drivers have to be meticulous about their pre-planning.

When I say go, you will choose a truck and try to find everything wrong. The first method of scoring will be finding everything. In the case of a tie, the second will be the time."

Everyone lined up as one of Gar's volunteers handed each a clipboard, pencil, and blank piece of paper. Stacie stood at the far end, and when the volunteer reached her, she glanced at Gar to see if she should give Stacie a clipboard.

Gar glared at Stacie, but she couldn't exactly say no. KayLynn had sat out for the first event and could still compete in the second.

She finally nodded, and Stacie took her clipboard from the volunteer's hand.

"Go!" Gar said.

Everyone ran toward the trucks, including Stacie.

"You really are magical with your healing," Katie said. "It's a good quality when you're surrounded by old people who tend to fall and hurt themselves."

"You're not old," I said.

Katie smiled. "Why don't you try to talk to Gar now? It seemed like this could take a while."

Volunteers surrounded Gar, but they didn't seem to be interacting much.

"Hi, Gardenia, is it?"

Gar winced. "Everyone calls me Gar."

"Sorry about that," I said. "Do you have a minute to chat about your ex-husband?"

"Are you a cop?" she looked me up and down. "I already talked to the cops."

"Nope, not a cop," I said. "I'm an independent news

reporter. I have millions of followers on social media who are fascinated with the Jubilant Jewel Jamboree and what happened with Randy."

"Is that all they're talking about?" Gar asked.

"I mean, I could sway them to talk about something else, but they're going to want to know who killed him."

"If I talk to you, will you do some positive advertising for the event? Our numbers are down, and if we don't get some people here in the next couple of days, we might have to cancel for next year."

"I think I can manage that." I felt terrible for lying to her. But maybe I could get Jake's fiancée, Georgia, to do a feature on one of her social media pages. She had lots of followers.

"What do you want to know?" She glanced around to make sure no one was listening.

"Who do you think killed him?" I asked.

"Stacie," she said without hesitation.

"Why would you think Stacie killed him?"

"She was engaged to him and didn't even seem to like him," Gar said. "I mean, other than when I found them together in my office. They seemed to like each other plenty at that moment."

My suspicion was that Gar only suspected Stacie because Stacie broke up her marriage.

"What about KayLynn or Bridget?"

"What about them?"

"Well, they were both sleeping with him, too."

Gar gaped at me. "KayLynn? Bridget?"

"I'm sorry, did you not know?"

Gar took a deep breath, but that didn't seem to calm her anger. "What else don't I know?"

Normally, I would have been pretty confident I could hold my own against this woman, but since I'd let myself get so out of shape, I took a step back. "Not much. Just that he seemed to be quite a player. Probably after the two of you divorced."

"But he was with KayLynn?"

"From what I can tell, yes."

"From what you can tell? Or you know?"

"KayLynn admitted it yesterday."

Her breath quickened as KayLynn came trotting back to the finish line with her clipboard and a smile.

"I'll kill that little rat for pretending to be my friend." Gar stomped away from me toward KayLynn.

KayLynn's smile quickly vanished when Gar ripped the clipboard out of her hand, yanked the paper from the top metal clasp, pulled out her knife, and sliced right through it.

"What was that for?" KayLynn asked.

Gar pointed the knife at her. "Did you sleep with my husband?"

"I—well—I—"

From behind me, a commotion took my attention from Gar and KayLynn.

"I am her attorney. You cannot arrest her." A man in a fancy suit and tie holding a briefcase was pleading with two police officers who had Emily in cuffs.

My head spun. So much was happening around me.

"You can meet us at the station," the scary officer from the day before said.

"Have you even read her the veranda rights?"

"Miranda," the officer said, then looked at Emily. "Maybe you should get yourself a better attorney."

Emily looked at the attorney, confused. "Can you meet us at the station?"

"I—uh—I can't drive," the attorney said. "My license got taken away because I drank alcohol."

The officer shook his head. "Not my problem."

"Don't tell them anything until I get there," the attorney said to Emily.

"I already told them everything last night," Emily said.

"That's enough," the police officer said. "Let's go."

18

The attorney took a step backward as the officer closed the car door with Emily in the back seat.

Gar had put the knife away when she'd seen the police but was still glaring at KayLynn.

I should have stayed, but everything told me to offer the attorney a ride to the police station. Maybe then I'd be able to get more information about the case.

"If you have a chance to talk to KayLynn, Bridget, or even the other two, go for it," I said to Katie. "Just be careful. Especially with Gar. My bets are on her being the murderer."

"Was that Emily they just put in the police car?" Katie asked. "Have you talked to her?"

"Where are you going?" Andrea said without letting me answer Katie's questions.

"I'm going to the police station. Feel free to come with me, but you have to sit in the back." I gave Katie a hug and a kiss on the cheek. "I'll tell you everything when I return."

Penelope followed as I approached the lawyer. "Do you need a ride down to the station?"

"Not from you," he said, crossing his arms over his chest.

"Uh, okay," I said. "I don't think we've ever met. I'm Ellie Vanderwick, and this is my pet pig, Penelope. I have a van, and we'd happily give you a ride."

The man's face softened when he looked down at Penelope.

She oinked up at him with her sweetest face, nose wiggle included.

"Fine," he said. "But we have to go right now."

"I parked my van in the lot," I said.

"Who is she, and why is she following us?" The attorney asked as we made our way out the event gates.

"She's a friend of mine," I said. "She doesn't like to be anywhere alone. She'll sit in the back. It'll be fine."

He eyed her with suspicion but didn't object.

"What's your name?" I asked.

"Why do you care so much about names?" the man practically shouted at me.

Now, I was thoroughly confused. "We haven't met before, right?"

"My name is George, okay?"

"George?"

"Yep."

"Well, it's nice to meet you, George." I stopped at Mona. "Here's our ride."

"This is your van?" The guy's eyes lit up, and a smile broached his lips before he realized he'd been smiling and quickly wiped it away. "I mean, it's kind of cool."

"Thanks," I said. "Her name is Mona. I've had her since I was sixteen."

"You bought a van when you were sixteen?"

"It's a long story," I said. "But yeah, kind of."

"Did you steal it?"

Andrea snickered in the back.

"No," I said. "I didn't steal it. I'm not a criminal if you're looking to pick up more clients."

"Oh, yeah, no, that's not what. I mean, sure, I like more clients. I love money."

I laughed. "Okay."

George reached down and patted Penelope as we drove out of the parking lot toward the police station. I'd been there several times, bailing out a boyfriend or two. My track record with men wasn't great.

Penelope looked like she was enjoying the attention.

"What's that?" I pointed at the tattoo that peeked out from beneath George's sleeve. "I've seen that tattoo before." It was the same one I'd seen on the burly guy who'd run me off when I was outside of the hotel.

He pulled his sleeve down to cover it. "It's nothing."

"It's a heart with a vine around it, right?"

"I said it's nothing."

"I bet it's a gang tattoo," Andrea said.

He turned and glared at her. "It is not. I'm not in a gang."

"Then tell us what it is."

"Make me."

"That's enough, children," I said with a laugh. "I was just curious. You don't have to tell me."

He didn't say anything else the entire ride, and when

we reached the police station, he hopped out without so much as a thank you. He did give Penelope one last pat on the head, though.

I put Mona in park and hurried up the steps of the police station behind him.

"Why are you following me? I can do this by myself."

"I trust that you can," I said. "But I have a few questions I'd like to ask the police. Is that okay with you?"

He didn't reply but pushed past me through the first set of doors, not bothering to hold the second one open for me.

What a jerk. I hoped this wasn't Emily's husband or boyfriend or Eloise's dad.

Eloise!

She was going to be at the jamboree all by herself. I could just imagine her going back to the food pavilion and finding her mother missing. Then someone telling her that her mother had been arrested.

I needed to go back.

But I wanted to talk to the police about whether they'd figured anything out on the case.

What were the chances they'd tell me anything? It wasn't like I was in Cliff Haven, where I'd proven myself to be a solid investigator. I was in Denver. These officers would laugh me out of the building.

I made my decision and turned to walk back out the doors.

"You're leaving?" George asked. "I thought you had questions."

"I have more important things to deal with," I said. "Will you need a ride somewhere after this?"

"No. I'll be fine."

"Then it was nice meeting you."

"Was it?"

I sighed. "Just do a good job for Miley. She deserves it."

He narrowed his eyes. "Oh, trust me. I will."

I turned back and walked outside, where Andrea waited for me on the sidewalk.

"I was just coming in," Andrea said.

"We need to get back to the jamboree. Now," I said.

"Why? What happened?"

"I'll explain everything on the ride over."

* * *

I told Andrea all about the conversation Xander and I had the night before. And then told her what Emily had said about Eloise.

"You have a sister?"

"I guess so," I said.

"That would make more sense as to why Xander is hesitant to break the spell without his father's help."

"Would it?"

"Magic is fickle, and Xander's right. Overloading her system with too much could cause permanent damage. You want your mother back, right?"

"Yes."

"Then be patient. At least you can rest knowing that she didn't abandon you. That she was actually protecting you."

Why hadn't I considered that? I'd been so worked up

about the Xander thing I hadn't even thought about the fact that my entire life story seemed like a lie. I'd stayed up night after night wondering why my mom wouldn't want me. Was it because of my hair? Did I scare her like I scared all the foster parents?

But in reality, she'd done something huge to protect me. She'd given up her entire life to protect me.

And now I was going to do whatever I could to protect her. And Eloise.

A tent full of massive statues and prizes for the truck judging competition replaced the trucks lined up at the front gate.

I hurried to the food pavilion but didn't see a little girl anywhere. Whether that meant she'd already been there and had left, or she was still oblivious to the fact that her mom was in jail at the moment, I didn't know.

"Have you seen a little girl about this tall with white curly hair?" I asked a man sitting at a table in the pavilion.

"Can't say I have."

I asked several other people who were eating, but no one had seen her.

Andrea had made her way from food stand to food stand, but she had come up empty-handed.

"Maybe that means she just hasn't come back to check in with her mother yet," I said. "I'll wait here with Penelope if you want to go tell Katie and the others that I'm back."

"I'm not leaving you here alone."

"I am perfectly fine," I said. "Plus, I need some time to think everything through. And make a phone call."

Andrea looked torn. "I'll be back in ten minutes. Don't go anywhere."

"Unless I see Eloise," I said.

"Fine, unless you see Eloise. But then bring her back to this table and wait until I get back."

"I will not kidnap my little sister."

"I'm not telling you to kidnap her. I'm telling you to persuade her to sit at this table for a couple of minutes and talk to you."

I huffed. "Fine."

When she was gone, I picked up my phone and called the Cliff Haven coroner's office. Neve answered on the second ring.

"Cliff Haven coroner, this is Neve."

"Hey, it's Ellie."

"Oh, hi! How are you? Did you find a body?" Neve was the only person who would sound excited about the prospect of me finding a body.

"Not in Cliff Haven," I said. "Are things slow there?"

"So slow," she said. "It's almost like before you came to town."

I laughed. There *had* been an uptick in murders since I'd moved to Cliff Haven. It was good that people liked me, or they might have run me out.

"Do you ever talk to other coroners?" I asked. "Would it be weird to call up another coroner in another state and ask them about their findings on a case?"

"An open case?"

"Yes."

"That's pretty tricky," she said. "Is this something you're working on? Where are you?"

"I'm in Denver."

"Iowa?"

"Colorado."

"Don't tell me you're thinking about moving back. We need you in Cliff Haven, even if you do bring the murderers out of the woodwork."

"I'm not moving," I said. "I love Cliff Haven. Don't say anything, especially to Jake, but my mother—Emily—is here and was arrested for murder. I need to find out the cause of death so I can clear her name."

"Is the case in Denver proper or a suburb?"

"It's in the City of Denver," I said.

"Perfect," she said. "I have a friend there who might help me out."

"Thanks, Neve. The guy's name is Randy Howard."

"Randy Howard. Got it. Talk to you later."

"Bye."

I put my phone back in my satchel and sighed. If the knife wound had been the cause of death, it would seal the deal for me that Gar had killed him. I'd just need a bit more evidence to prove it to the police. Maybe George would help. He didn't seem to like me much, but if it would help his case, he'd only be smart to help, right?

"What are you doing sitting over here?" Katie asked. "The judging is happening!"

She pulled me to a stand.

"Go ahead," Andrea said. "I'll monitor things here. If I see—uh—anything, I'll let you know right away."

I'd really wanted it to be me who was there when

Eloise showed up. Like maybe we'd have some kind of instant connection or something.

"Don't—uh—do anything until I'm back," I said.

"I'll just observe," Andrea said as if understanding what I meant.

"That was very cryptic," Katie said as we started toward the trucks.

"They arrested Emily, as you saw," I said. "But I just found out she has a daughter—another daughter."

Katie gasped exactly as a good friend did in a situation like this.

"She's only nine," I said. "I can't imagine how freaked out she'll be when she shows up at the food pavilion looking for her mom only to find out Emily—Miley—has been arrested and taken to jail."

"Does she have a dad?" Katie asked, then shook her head. "I don't mean like does she have a dad, but is her dad in the picture? Maybe she won't be as freaked out as you think if she has a father figure to lean on."

I hadn't considered that. I had considered that maybe George could have been her dad. Or maybe her dad has something to do with that tattoo that everyone around Emily seemed to have. What if her father was the head of some gang or mafia or something?

"Stop spiraling," Katie said, wrapping an arm around my back and squeezing me tight to her side. "We'll get it all figured out, whether she has a dad or not."

"Thanks," I said.

Katie looked around at the trucks. We were halfway down the first row, surrounded by shiny chrome, bright colors, and many interesting characters.

Penelope stopped to meet a toy poodle wearing a tiny leather jacket that matched the woman I assumed owned the big blue truck in front of us.

"This is a beautiful truck," Katie said.

"And such a cute little doggie." I let the pup smell my outstretched hand.

"Thank you," the woman said with a deep southern accent. "Don't think the judges thought much about it. They were too focused on that one over there."

I followed where she pointed to a truck across the aisle and about five trucks up.

"What's so special about that one?" I asked.

"Nothing," the woman said. "Except who owns it."

"Let me guess," I said. "Gar Howard?"

"Smart cookie," she said. "The contest is rigged. One of her trucks wins every year. Granted, she owns over fifty percent of the trucks and runs the event."

"How does she keep the business running with so many trucks out of operation for this event?" I asked.

"She has so many trucks. This is like a drop in the bucket to her. And now that Randy is out of the way, she's probably one of the wealthiest women in America. I hear a few here aren't too pleased about all that, either."

"Like the women Randy was dating?"

"And engaged to," the woman said. "But they'd be foolish to take on Gar. She'd bury them so deep they'd wish they were dead."

"Do you think it's possible she killed someone?" Katie asked. "Such as her ex-husband?"

"If I thought anyone could kill someone, it would be her."

20

Another person suspecting Gar as the killer was great, especially since this truck driver didn't seem to be so closely related. The only problem was, other than the knife she kept in her pocket and waved around when she was threatened, there wasn't much tying her to the murder. Not that I knew of, anyway.

Other than motive—there was plenty of motive between the money and the business, and Randy sleeping with practically every woman under the sun.

We thanked the woman and patted the poodle one more time before moving onto another truck.

"Do you think it's Gar?" Katie asked when we were out of earshot.

"I'm leaning that way," I said. "But I don't know. If only I knew how he died, I might make some sort of inference."

"Wasn't he stabbed?" Katie asked.

"Yes, but it looked like there may have been gunshot

wounds, too," I said. "Maybe the knife was just a distraction."

If that was the case, my entire theory of it being Gar because of her knife-toting ways was blown to bits.

I checked my cell phone to see if Neve had already gotten back to me.

No such luck.

The judges were busy talking to Stacie when we walked up to her truck. Hers was more of a house on wheels that could hook up to a big trailer. Currently, she had what looked like a trailer that would tow race cars or something.

"Can we see inside?" one of the judges asked Stacie.

"Of course," Stacie said, then looked at Katie and me. "You can come in too."

We walked up the metal steps and into what was almost like an upgraded Mona interior. Like way upgraded.

A large bed at the back had black silk privacy curtains pulled back and fastened with skull clips attached to each wall.

The kitchen was meticulous, with everything in its place and secured for movement.

"I keep the utensils in here," she said, quickly opening and closing the drawer flashing perfect lines of forks, knives, and spoons. "The pots and pans are in this cabinet, and my dishes are up here."

As she continued to try to impress the judges, I looked around at the rest of the setup. The white carpet had a few minor stains at the edges, probably too set in to get out, and one of the cushions on the convertible couch bed had a small tear on the top. Otherwise, everything was pristine. It didn't even look lived in.

Though, I suppose that was the whole point of the contest—having the nicest truck inside and out.

The judges made a few notes on their clipboards and then returned outside.

Stacie followed, leaving Katie and me inside.

"This is really nice," Katie said. "Do you think this is where she invites all her fiancés?"

I laughed. "Maybe, but you'd never know it with how clean everything is."

"It's kind of creepy, though, with all the skulls."

I'd only noticed the curtain clips, but now that I looked around a bit more, Katie was right. Almost everything had a skull on it. Even the black cushions had raised black skulls that were only easy to see if you were up close.

"Do you think she's part of a cult or something?" Katie asked.

"Speaking of cults, or gangs, or mafia, I don't know. But have you ever seen a tattoo of a heart with a vine wrapped around it?"

Katie and I stepped out of the truck onto the concrete. "Can't say I have. Why?"

"I've just come into contact with two men who each had the tattoo and were both closely associated with Emily."

"Have you checked the Google?"

I did a mental head slap. Of course! I could use the internet like a real detective would. "I'll do that as soon as we talk to the other two."

Stacie was still trying to wow the judges, so we moved on to Bridget's bright red truck.

Not shockingly, Nancy was ogling the truck. She definitely had a thing for red.

But Bridget also seemed to be opening up to Nancy. Which made sense because Nancy was about the sweetest woman in the entire world.

"So you don't think Miley killed Randy?" Nancy asked as Katie, and I walked up.

Bridget glanced at us with a worried expression.

"Don't worry about them," Nancy said. "They're my friends."

Bridget hesitated but then nodded. "Yeah, I don't think she did it. I think Gar did. But everyone else said Miley did, so I went along."

"Why?" I asked.

"Because I didn't want the cops to think it was me."

"And why would they think it was you?" Nancy asked. "You're such a sweetheart. I can't imagine anyone would take you as a murderer."

Bridget winced at the word murderer. "I had a relationship with him. And I knew he was with other women, but maybe they'd think I killed him because I was jealous."

"It would only be natural to be jealous," Nancy said. "I don't know what I'd do if Hank cheated with another woman."

Katie laughed. "He's only got eyes for you. Don't you worry."

"That must be nice," Bridget said. "I don't think I've ever been with a man who only had eyes for me. My mom said it was because I was too bland. Too normal."

"You're not bland," I said. "I think you're very pretty."

"You do?" Bridget's eyes filled up with tears. "Are you just saying that to be nice?"

"Not at all," I said. "Your hair is so pretty, and your eyes are stunning. You should push your hair out of your face more often so people can see them."

She pushed her hair back.

"That's better." I smiled. "Do you know if Gar was with Randy the night he was murdered?"

She looked like I'd socked her in the stomach. "I—I don't know. I think my turn is coming. I better shine my truck."

Nancy put a hand on Bridget's back, and, by the way Bridget relaxed, you'd think Nancy was the one with healing magic. "It's okay. You can tell us."

Bridget's body started shaking. "I know she did it. I saw her."

21

Nancy, Katie, and I stared at Bridget for a heavy second. Even Penelope waited for the rest of the story.

"What do you mean you saw her?" Nancy asked. "You saw Gar kill Randy?"

Bridget nodded. "They were together in the food pavilion around midnight. I went over for a midnight snack, but when I saw them holding hands, I hid to see what else might happen."

Katie started to ask another question, but I placed a hand on her arm. If we gave Bridget some space and silence to talk, she'd probably tell us more than if we asked her questions.

As I suspected, she continued, "After a while, their gentleness turned to anger. No one else was around. Miley had gone off to take the trash to the dumpster on the other side of the lot. She must have left the door to her stall unlocked because that's where Gar and Randy disappeared. After what sounded like arguing and a physical fight, Gar hurried out and took off running. All I could see were Randy's cowboy boots sticking out the door."

"Did Miley go back and find him?" I asked, unable to continue sitting in silence.

"I don't know. I didn't want to stick around and get accused of doing anything. I figured she would have called it in right away if she did. But then morning came, and I still hadn't heard about it—I figured Stacie would be the first to know since she had the ring and all. I eventually went down to the pavilion to check it out, but nothing was happening. When I peeked around the side, his boots were still sticking out the door. I worried that Miley had been hurt too, but I didn't know where to look for her. So I came back to my truck and waited. Eventually, Stacie came and told me."

"Stacie came and told you?" I asked.

"Yeah, she told me," Bridget said, her eyes moving around as if trying to get her story straight. "I acted like I was surprised."

"Did the police talk to you about any of this?" I asked.

She nodded. "But I didn't tell them about Gar. I didn't want her to try to kill me, too. I know they talked to Gar, Stacie, and KayLynn. And now they have Miley in jail. I mean, maybe Miley killed him, you know? Maybe Gar knocked him out, and Miley went in there and finished the job after I was gone. I don't know."

"How was Stacie when she told you he was dead?"

"She was sobbing and shouting when she pounded on my door," Bridget said.

That differed from how she'd acted at the scene.

"And how did Gar and KayLynn find out he was dead?"

I asked. "It seemed like you all got there around the same time."

Bridget glanced around with a look of fear in her eyes.

"We won't tell the police, Gar, or anyone," Nancy lied. "We just want to make sure you're okay. And sometimes talking about things can help."

She was good. I needed to use her more often when I talked to suspects. Not that I wanted there to be any more need for her sweet-talking ways, but who was I kidding? There would likely be murders around me until I was dead myself.

"KayLynn's truck is right next to mine." She motioned to the truck on the other side. "So she heard Stacie freaking out, you know? And she came out and demanded we tell her what was happening."

"So Stacie told her?" Nancy asked.

"Yeah," Bridget said. "I don't know how Gar found out. Probably through her minions."

She was the event planner, so it was likely if a body were found at her event, she'd be one of the first to know.

"Do you know what Stacie told the police? Did she have an alibi for that night?"

"I don't know," Bridget said. "You should ask her that."

I did, and she wouldn't tell me.

"So if Gar did kill him, how do you think she did it?"

"Probably with her knife," Bridget said. "The one she carries around with her everywhere."

"But she had it after the murder," I said.

Bridget shrugged. "She probably has more than one."

"Do you know what her knives look like? Maybe I can compare it to the picture I have."

"You have pictures of the crime scene?" Bridget asked. "Can I see them?"

I hesitated. "Why? Do you really want to see him like that?"

"I—uh—maybe it'll help me heal or whatever. Bring closure or something."

I pulled my phone from my bag, unlocked the screen, and opened the photos app.

Not trusting her, I held onto the phone while she scrolled through. Her eyes were wide. "This is horrible. How did you get these?"

I hadn't considered she'd ask me that question.

"I know the police," I lied.

"So, the police have these photos?"

"Um, no," I said. "I have been meaning to send them to my contact but just haven't gotten around to it. They probably have their own photos, though."

"Right, you're probably right," she said. "That's good."

My phone vibrated in my hand as Bridget swiped to the next photo.

"Oh shoot, I think I deleted them," Bridget said.

I whipped my phone around to look. Sure enough, the photos of the crime scene were gone. I swiped and swiped, but the only pictures left were pictures of Penelope.

"I am so sorry," Bridget said. "I don't know how that could even happen. Is there a way to get them back?"

I'd only recently gotten a smartphone and didn't know

all the ins and outs of it yet. "I don't know." I tapped a few buttons, but nothing came up.

"I'm sure that contact you have at the police department will get them back for you, right?" Bridget looked like she was about to cry. "I feel horrible. I'm so, so sorry."

"It'll be fine," I said. "It's not a big deal."

But it was a big deal. A really big deal.

22

Bridget offered to give me money or to take my phone to a phone guy she knew to see if he could get the pictures back, but there was no way I was letting anyone else touch my phone again.

Sure, I'd lost some crime scene photos. But if I lost all my fun pictures with Penelope, I'd be heartbroken.

Maybe I needed to figure out a way to back everything up, so things like this didn't happen again.

We walked away as Bridget continued to apologize.

"Maybe it's not a big deal," Nancy said. "I mean, if she saw Gar kill him, then we know who did it anyway, right?"

When we were about two steps from KayLynn's truck, Katie stopped us. "Give me your phone."

"Why?" I asked.

"Just trust me," she said. "Melody taught me a trick."

Melody was Katie's movie star daughter.

I unlocked the phone and handed it over to her. "Just try not to delete the pictures of Penelope and me."

"Don't you have it backed up to the sky?" Katie asked.

"It's the cloud," Nancy corrected.

"No," I said. "But I should."

"We'll get Earl to figure it out when we get back to Cliff Haven. He's much more tech-savvy than me. I think that's where Melody gets it," Katie said with a smile.

Or maybe she got it from the fact that it was nearly impossible to be my age and not know how to use technology. Unless you grew up without it. It wasn't until the past year that I could even afford anything other than an old flip phone.

"There, your pictures have been restored," Katie said, handing the phone back to me.

Sure enough, all the crime scene photos were back in my camera roll. "How did you do that?"

"These phones don't delete anything for good unless you do it twice. It's annoying if you ask me. But I guess in instances like this, it's a nice feature." She tapped a few times on my screen and pulled up a folder called deleted photos. "They were in there."

Also, there were all the horrible pictures I'd taken of myself and deleted. I quickly backed out of that album. "Thanks."

"Do you think she did it on purpose?" Katie asked.

"She seemed genuinely upset that she'd done it," Nancy said.

"And I think her finger slipped when my phone vibrated." My mind went back to the notification. "Why did my phone vibrate, anyway?"

Katie pointed to a red circle with a number one above

my messaging app. "Probably because you have a text message."

I sighed. I at least knew that much when it came to working my phone.

I tapped on the messages app and pulled up a text from Xander.

XANDER

Still haven't found him. All good there?

I typed out a quick reply.

Miley was arrested. I just found out I have a sister. Anything else you haven't told me?

His response was immediate.

Are you with Eloise right now?

No, I don't know where she is.

I'm on my way.

Even though he hadn't answered my question, I still wanted him here. Something about his presence, even when I was furious with him, made everything seem more normal—safer. Maybe that was because he had been my guardian.

"Should we go chat with KayLynn?" Katie asked, pointing to the bright pink truck in front of us with KayLynn's name scrawled across the side in calligraphy-style letters.

I led the way to the driver's side door, but just as I was

about to knock, I heard someone throwing up near the back of the trailer.

I looked back at Katie and Nancy, who both shrugged.

Carefully, I walked toward the sound to find KayLynn hunched over, vomiting all over the ground.

"Oh wow," I said, trying not to vomit myself. "Are you okay?"

"Does it look like I'm okay?" KayLynn asked, then threw up again. "I just drank too much last night."

"And it's only now catching up to you?"

I wasn't a big drinker, but I was pretty confident you rarely threw up more than eighteen hours after you'd gotten drunk.

"Maybe I should take you to the hospital. You could have alcohol poisoning."

"I've been drinking all day, okay? Just leave me alone." KayLynn wiped her mouth with a lace handkerchief. "Why aren't you leaving?"

"You weren't drunk all day," I said. "You won the scavenger hunt. If you'd been drinking, you wouldn't have won."

"It was rigged for me to win," KayLynn said. "Until Gar found out I had been sleeping with her dead ex-husband."

This was the first time I realized I didn't know who'd won the Olympic competition since I'd left in such a hurry to go to the police station.

"Who won then?" I asked.

"Some no-name," KayLynn said with a shrug.

"Are you going to be okay to show off your truck?" I asked.

"Why wouldn't I be?" KayLynn asked. "Do you think this is the first time I've puked? I know how to take care of myself. I've been doing it my whole life."

I almost told her I had too, but that wasn't entirely true. Even though my foster families had dropped me the moment my hair changed, they'd still taken care of me up to that point. Well, most of them, anyway.

Plus, someone had apparently been creating magical spaces for me without my knowledge.

"When did you find out that Randy was dead?" I asked.

"At the food pavilion." She retched again. "Don't remind me. I can't even think of that at a time like this."

"Are you sure that's when you found out?"

She stood and looked me directly in the eyes. "Are you calling me a liar?"

"No," I said. "But I have information that you knew he was dead before you went over there. That you were faking shock."

"Then I must be a world-class actress. Too bad Hollywood's not knocking on my door. Is that all?"

I was getting nowhere with this line of questioning.

"Who do you think killed Randy?"

"Miley," she said. "She poisoned him with her pancakes."

"How do you know for sure?"

"It's the only possibility."

"What if I told you he didn't die of poisoning? He died of a stab wound?"

"Then I'd say Miley stabbed him," KayLynn said. "Didn't the police already arrest her?"

"Yes."

"Then why are you out here poking your head where it don't belong?"

"I don't think she did it."

"Do you know Miley?"

"Not really."

"Then let me give you a little lesson." She dabbed the handkerchief over her mouth again. "Miley might look pretty and sweet, but there's more to her than she lets on. And that daughter of hers is nothing but trouble. I'd say she was probably in on it."

"The nine-year-old daughter?" I asked. "You think she helped her mother kill a man?"

"It's entirely possible."

I shook my head and moved on. "Did Miley have any reason to kill Randy?"

"They dated a while back," KayLynn said. "Maybe he's the father of her child. Who knows? Either way, she got what she deserved. You can't just go around killing people."

Before I could ask her another question, she vomited all over my pants.

23

I'd have given almost anything for one pair of the perfect pants from that perfect wardrobe in that perfect Hotel Wix room.

No amount of water could get the stink off my pants. Whatever KayLynn had eaten, it had made her vomit bright orange.

"It's really not that bad," Nancy tried to reassure me. "I can hardly smell it."

"That's because you're not downwind," Katie said, her voice higher pitched because she was holding her nose.

"You're just being a dramatic old lady," Nancy said.

"Who are you calling old?" Katie said.

"Okay, okay, that's enough," I said with a laugh. "There's been enough girl fighting for my liking lately."

Fran and Amy were at the food pavilion with Andrea when we returned.

"Still no sign of Eloise?" I asked.

Andrea shook her head. "Maybe someone she knew took her to the police station."

"Who's Eloise?" Fran asked.

I took a few minutes to fill them in on everything that was going on and how we couldn't talk to Emily like she was Emily but that we had to treat her like Miley—someone we'd only just met.

If we ever got to see her again.

I stopped myself.

No.

I couldn't have a negative mindset.

We were going to see her. We were going to get her out of jail. We were going to fix her brain, bring back her memories, and bring her and Eloise back to Cliff Haven, where they belonged.

"We should go down there and tell them about Gar," Nancy said. "They might not let Emily go just because we tell them that, but at least they'd be looking in another direction besides Emily's."

"And we could check if Eloise is there, too," Katie said.

The sun was dropping below the horizon, and the judging had concluded for the day. The lights on the trucks were beautiful against the orange and blue sky.

"I think that's the best we can do right now," I said. "And if you guys don't want to come, I can drop you off at the hotel, and Andrea and I can just head down there."

"There's no way you're not taking us," Nancy said. "We roll together. Like a group of rollie-pollies."

Amy laughed. "Then let's roll out."

The sky was dark by the time we arrived at the police station. The door had a sign that said we had to buzz in on the intercom to speak to someone.

I pushed the silver button and waited for a voice from the attached speaker.

Instead, a buzzing sound followed by a click indicated the door had been unlocked.

Apparently, they didn't think we—yes, all of us—were criminals ready to take over the police station.

A police officer met us in the lobby. "Can I help you, ladies?"

"Why, yes, you can," Nancy said, batting her eyelashes at the handsome man. "We have some information about a murder."

I couldn't tell whether it was the excitement or nervousness that danced in his eyes. "Why don't you come back to a meeting room, and I can take some notes?"

He led us through a set of locked doors to a meeting room with a long table down the center surrounded by comfy chairs on wheels.

"Please, have a seat," he pulled the chair out for Nancy.

"Oh, you are quite the gentleman," she gushed.

He smiled at me as he helped push her chair closer to the table.

My scalp tingled, but I wouldn't let my hair change right now. That would just complicate the situation. Plus, he could smile at me like that as much as he wanted. He had a nice smile.

"Now, tell me what you know," he said to Nancy as he took the seat next to her.

"Oh, you're too kind to think I'd be the one to divulge the information," Nancy flirted. "But you should really talk to our private detective over there. Ellie, will you tell him?"

I laughed nervously. "I'm not a private detective."

The officer turned toward me and smiled. "I'd love to hear what you know."

"There was a murder at the Jubilant Jewel Jamboree—Randy Howard."

"I'm aware of the situation," he said. "We have a suspect in custody."

"Yes," I said. "I know. But I think you have the wrong woman."

He tilted his head in amusement. He didn't seem to take me seriously, but at least he was still listening.

"I believe the person who murdered Randy was his ex-wife, Gardenia Howard. She goes by Gar."

"One of our officers spoke with her," he said. "She had a solid alibi for the entire evening."

"What was the alibi?"

"She said she did have dinner with Randy, but then they parted ways, and she went to a midnight showing of the new superhero movie. We confirmed all of it with video, cell phones, and receipts. She's not the killer."

"Do you think she could have killed him before she went to the movie?" I asked.

"I don't think anything," he said. "I only go by the facts. And the coroner said Randy died between the hours of one and three in the morning. That movie didn't end until half-past three. Like I said, her alibi is solid."

"Did the coroner say how he died?"

The officer narrowed his eyes at me but kept a smile on his lips. "You sure you're not a private detective?"

"I'm just interested in the case, is all," I said.

"Why do you think Gar did it?"

"There was a witness who saw them together, saw them argue, saw them go into the food stall, then heard a bunch of banging noises before she found his feet poking out of the door."

"And why hasn't this witness come forward?" he asked, his tone on the verge of mocking me.

"She thinks if she comes forward, the police will suspect her of committing the crime, or she might be in danger."

"Does she now?" He leaned forward, resting his hands on the table. "Why would she think that?"

The way he asked told me he thought I was this witness. "Oh no. I'm not the witness. I wasn't even in the state when all of this happened."

"So, you've been questioning people?"

Ah, he had me there.

"Just asking around."

"Why?"

I couldn't tell him the truth.

All the women watched as I tried to come up with a plausible reason other than Miley is actually Emily, who is my mom, but she doesn't know it because she has some sort of magical amnesia.

But before I came up with anything, the officer's face changed.

He held up a finger for me not to say anything as he grabbed for the mic clipped on top of his shoulder.

"Copy, I'm on my way."

The officer stood. "I'm sorry to cut this meeting short, but I have a matter of urgency to attend to."

"Will you at least look into Gar? Go talk to her one more time?" I asked, my voice more pleading than I wanted it to be.

"I'm sorry, I can't do that."

I grabbed his arm, and he turned to look at me.

"Please," I said. "Just talk to her."

He softened. "It's not that I don't want to. I can't because she's dead."

24

Chaos broke out when Nancy, Katie, Amy, Fran, and Andrea heard him say Gar was dead. They were all speaking at once.

"What do you mean she's dead?" Nancy asked.

"Did she die the same way as Randy?" Katie asked.

"It was Stacie," Fran said. "Stacie hates her."

"Or Bridget," Amy said.

"KayLynn could have done it, too," I chimed in.

The officer let out a loud whistle. "I have to leave now. There might be a murderer on the loose. But you have to get out of the police station in order for me to leave. Now, let's go."

His forceful tone was almost sexy.

Apparently, I wasn't the only one who thought so because Nancy and Katie were both gawking at him.

"Come on." He held open the door, so we could all file out.

I was the last to walk past him.

"I know you mean well, but leave this to the professionals. I wouldn't want you to get hurt." He winked and closed the station doors behind him, pulling once to ensure they were locked before hopping into his patrol car and driving off.

"He likes you," Fran teased.

"He's not terrible on the eyes," Katie said as they hopped into Mona.

Penelope was asleep in the driver's seat but woke when I opened my door. "I don't need a man telling me to stay out of trouble lest I get hurt. That seems chauvinistic, don't you think?"

"Or chivalrous," Nancy said with a dramatic sigh.

I lifted Penelope off the seat and carefully placed her on the pillow on the floor.

"If Gar is dead," I said, moving away from the discussion about the hunky cop, "does that mean she didn't kill Randy after all?"

"Or someone found out she did kill him and killed her," Amy said.

"This just made everything way more complicated." I backed out of the spot and turned in the direction of the jamboree.

"Where are we going?" Andrea asked.

"Back to the jamboree," I said. "Unless anyone wants me to take them to the hotel really quick?"

No one said a word.

"Good." I tickled the dash. "To the jamboree, please, Mona."

We got there so quickly we beat Mr. Hunky Officer.

"Don't let him see you," I said. "If he finds out we beat him here, he'll be suspicious."

"Yeah, and if he thinks you're a witch, he might not even ask you out," Fran said.

Amy jabbed her in the ribs.

"What? It's true." Fran held her hands up.

The crappy part was it was true. Only two men had accepted me as a witch, and they were both warlocks.

"It's fine," I said. "I'm not interested, anyway."

"Uh-huh, sure you're not," Fran said, wiggling her eyebrows.

A crowd had gathered at the jamboree entrance.

I hurried through the people, weaving my way through until I got to the scene.

Gar was on her back. There was no blood around her on the ground, but there was some on her blouse where it looked like she might have been stabbed. I couldn't see a knife anywhere.

I pulled out my phone and snapped pictures just in case I had to hightail it out of there so the hunky cop didn't see me.

An older woman with a tight gray bun on top of her head grabbed my arm. "Why are you taking pictures?"

"I'm just, it's nothing, I—"

Before I could assure her this wasn't a big deal, she started screaming. "She's taking pictures of a dead body to put on social media!"

I tried to pull my hand out of hers, but she had a tight grip.

Her hand was wrinkled, but in the crook between her thumb and her pointer finger was the same tattoo I'd seen on two other people—the heart with the vine.

"What is that tattoo?" I asked.

She looked down at where I pointed on her hand, gasped, and let me go.

Before she could explain or grab me again, I took off running.

When I got to the event gates, I ran smack into Mr. Hunky Cop himself.

As he stumbled backward, I let my hair change color, the effect happening instantly.

The long white hair hanging in a braid over my shoulder unraveled into bright red waves.

"Sorry," I said, trying to keep my face covered.

He tilted his head sideways to get a better look at me. "Do I know you from somewhere?"

"Nope," I said, trying to lower my voice. "I don't know any cops—I mean—officers."

He looked torn. He needed to get inside and secure the crime scene, but seeing me threw him.

"I need to go," I said and strode out of the gate and away from where I'd parked Mona. If he followed me, Mona would be a dead giveaway.

"Did you see a girl with bright white hair run out here?" A voice asked from behind me. It was the older woman with the tattoo. "She was taking pictures of the dead body to post on social media."

I kept walking. She obviously hadn't seen my clothes because changing anything about my appearance besides my hair was beyond my abilities.

"No," he finally said. "But we have more important things to worry about than some true-crime-obsessed freak."

I was about to turn a corner toward the hotel where Emily had been staying when I peeked over my shoulder.

The officer had already disappeared from view, but the older woman stood at the gate searching the area.

When our gazes met, I couldn't look away fast enough.

Her eyes widened, and she started screaming again.

But this time, no one seemed to listen, and even if they were, I would have liked to see them try to catch me.

25

"Do you think it's obvious enough that Emily didn't kill anyone?" I asked my friends when I got back to Mona. "From the looks of things, Gar was stabbed too, but the knife wasn't stuck in her chest or anywhere I could see."

"I don't know if that's enough to get Emily off the hook," Fran said. "But I'm sure the police know more about the details than we do."

That reminded me. I still hadn't heard from Neve or Xander.

"Can someone call my phone and make sure it's working?" I asked.

Katie called, and sure enough, it rang.

"That's so strange," I said.

"Who are you waiting to hear from?" Amy asked.

"Xander, for one," I said. "When I told him Emily went to jail and Eloise was out there somewhere, presumably alone, he said he'd be coming back straight away. But also from Neve. She told me she might be able to get me some details on the case."

I looked down at my phone. It was too late to call her, but I sent a quick text.

> Any news? We have another body. Looks to be similar.

I didn't expect to hear from her before morning, but my phone dinged within a few seconds of sending it.

NEVE

> Results are inconclusive so far. There are too many possibilities. Stab wound to the chest, gunshots in the arm, poison in the system, and suffocation. The knife wound doesn't match the knife that was in the wound. Tell me more about the new victim.

I relayed the information to the others. While they mulled it over, I replied to Neve.

> Here's a picture. It's kind of dark, but maybe you can see something I don't.

I sent the best picture I'd got from the scene.

> No blood on the ground, but it looks like a stab wound to the chest, for sure.

The three bubbles showing she was responding appeared. Then disappeared. Appeared again. Then disappeared.

I waited for a response to come in. Sometimes, if it was a long one, it took a couple of seconds after the bubbles stopped, but nothing came. I sent one more message.

Any ideas?

This time, there were no bubbles. Surely, she hadn't fallen asleep right in the middle of texting me, right?

"Ellie?" Katie said from the back.

I turned around. "Did you think of something?"

She shook her head and pointed out the windshield.

I spun around to look at where she was pointing.

Three people were walking up to one of the motel room doors—Emily, Xander, and a nine-year-old girl —Eloise.

I swallowed. Why wouldn't he have called me and told me he had found Eloise and that Emily had been released?

Emily pulled a keycard from her purse as they approached the door while Eloise hopped around with excitement in front of Xander.

She spun around and then grabbed both of his hands and swung their arms like they were dancing. I couldn't see his face, but he seemed at ease with the situation. Almost like—

I stopped my train of thought in its tracks.

There was no way. They weren't a family. He told me he hadn't dated Emily. That they were more like brother and sister. He couldn't possibly be Eloise's father. Could he?

I was about to have Mona take us back to our hotel when Xander turned around and instantly spotted me.

Eloise tried to get his attention back on her as Emily opened the door and walked into the room.

Xander looked torn. I'm sure he could see the confusion in my eyes.

But Eloise was pulling him toward the door.

He frowned.

Eloise looked past him at what he might be more interested in than her. Her gaze found me within seconds. She narrowed her eyes at me, then looked up at Xander and said something.

If only I could read lips.

Whatever it was, it caused him to follow her inside the motel room and close the door behind them.

I tickled Mona's dash and told her to take us to our hotel.

***

"Come on, talk to us," Nancy said.

I wrapped myself in a blanket on the fancy couch while cheesy romance movies played on the TV in the background.

"There's nothing to say," I said. "Emily is out of harm's way. She doesn't seem to be a suspect anymore. So, I'm done with this case. We can go home first thing tomorrow morning."

"What about Xander?" Amy asked gently.

I shrugged. "What about him? His life is none of my business. And Emily—Miley—isn't even really my mom. She doesn't remember me. So, things can just go back to the way they were before. I'll go back to Cliff Haven and live my awesome magical life with my awesome friends, my awesome pig in my awesome house, and my awesome Mona. I have such a good life there. I don't know why I was searching for anything else, anyway."

Katie wrapped an arm around my shoulder. "It's only natural that you'd want to find your parents. Especially after the childhood you had. But I assure you, you have all the mothers and grandmothers you need in Cliff Haven. We love you like you're one of our own. And Jake does too."

"We can't tell Jake about any of this," I said. "If he knows where Emily is, he'll for sure overwhelm her brain."

"You might be surprised," Fran said. "He and Georgia seem to be pretty happy together."

I shook my head. "That's exactly why we shouldn't tell him. There's no need to make him feel like I do now." I'd done so well keeping my emotions back, but admitting aloud that I had feelings about it brought down my wall, and the tears spilled out.

"Oh, sweetie," Katie cooed. "It's okay. I know this is hard, but everything will be fine. We'll get home, and you can investigate murders with Jake again, and life will get back to normal."

"Well, other than the fact that you'll be the Grand Witch of the States," Andrea said.

This made me sob louder.

"Andrea," Fran said. "You need to learn when to keep your inner thoughts to yourself."

Some of me had been hoping that when we found Emily, she would take the position, and I'd be off the hook. Part of being off the hook, though, was so Xander and I could have had a chance together.

Even that seemed implausible now. He'd lied too much.

Penelope wiggled her snout on my cheek, giving me kisses.

I pulled her closer to me and cried harder.

"Crying is good," Katie said. "Let it all out."

"Actually, you need to stop," Andrea said. "Xander is here."

26

I pulled Penelope to me tighter. "I don't want to see him."

"You don't have an option," Andrea said. "He's a council member, and you're obliged to take meetings from council members."

"I am not the Grand Witch yet," I said. "Have him talk to Renée."

"Renée is busy," Andrea said.

"Is this official business or personal?" Katie asked.

"Official," Andrea said. "Go clean yourself up before he comes in."

"Let him in," I said. "I don't need to clean myself up."

Andrea shrugged, and the elevator doors opened as if on cue, revealing a tired-looking Xander.

"Ellie." He hurried to my side and sat on the couch next to me.

Both Penelope and Katie let out grumbly sounds.

Xander scooted back away from me slightly. "I need to talk to you."

"Andrea said it was official business," I said, wiping tears off my cheeks. "What official business could you possibly need to discuss with me at this moment?"

"We need to figure out who killed Gar and Randy," he said. "The council thinks whoever did it was trying to kill Miley."

His calling her Miley made my chest constrict.

"That's about the dumbest thing I've ever heard the council come up with," I said. "Emily was in jail when Gar was killed. If they'd been trying to kill Emily, they would have had to get inside the jail to do so."

"Or get her out," Xander said.

Shoot. He had a point.

"The only way to get her out was to kill someone else and make it look the same as the first murder, so Mi—Emily—would be released."

"Then why are you here?" I asked. "Why aren't you out there protecting her?"

"She has plenty of protection," Xander said. "Trust me."

"All those people with the heart and vine tattoos?" I asked. "Like the woman who tried to get me arrested for taking pictures of the crime scene? Or the man who threatened me if I didn't stop watching her. Or her ridiculously inept attorney?"

Xander looked at me, confused. "Maybe," he said slowly.

"Fine," I said. "So, she's protected. Why don't you work with the police to find out who did it? The murderer didn't kill them with magic, right?"

"The magical medical examiner doesn't think so."

"So, someone non-magical is trying to kill Emily?" I shook my head. "Why?"

"Why does anyone kill anyone else?" Xander asked.

"Money? Love? Fear? Jealousy? Rage?" I said. "There are lots of reasons people kill other people. So, which is it?"

"That's what we have to figure out," Xander said.

I shook my head. "If she's being protected and the person who is killing others isn't magical, then I don't need to be in the middle of this. I'm going back to Cliff Haven tomorrow. This chapter of my life is closed. Emily—Miley—and Eloise can have their happily ever after life without me, and I'll have mine without them."

I stopped myself from adding Xander to Emily and Eloise's happily ever after. That was one conversation I didn't want to have. Especially not in front of all of my friends.

"But what if my dad—"

"If your dad could have fixed this—or wanted to fix this—he would have done so by now. He told me to stay away. Why else would he want to leave Miley as Miley?"

"I think she might know something about his past that he doesn't want anyone else to know," Xander said. "If her memory comes back, everything could change for him."

"Hasn't the council been looking for him for years? They haven't found him. What makes him think if Emily gets her memories back, they'll magically be able to find him?"

Xander ran a hand over his beard. "I don't know. All I know is I need your help. I need you."

He reached for my hand, but Penelope snapped at him, and he jerked it back.

She'd never been fond of us getting close.

"How do you think I can help?" I asked, ignoring the sentiment that he needed me.

"You have a way with these things," Xander said. "You can sense when someone is lying—their emotions. You've solved more cases than anyone I know. Magical or otherwise."

I glanced around at all the women waiting to hear my answer. "Do you guys think I could have a few minutes with Xander alone?"

That was all I had to say before they hopped up and marched out of the room.

"You said you were going to tell me the truth about everything," I said. "Why didn't you call and tell me that Emily was out of jail? Or that I had a sister? Or that you'd found my sister?"

"I did," Xander said. "I left you messages—a bunch of them. I just thought you didn't want to talk to me."

I pulled my phone out of my satchel and showed him the screen.

"May I?" He held out a hand.

Still on my lap, Penelope looked up at me and waited for my answer.

I unlocked it and handed him the phone.

He immediately went to my voicemail box. "Hmmm . . ." He ran a finger along the side of the screen. "Has someone else touched this recently? Someone magical?"

I thought back. "Bridget did. But she's not magical, as far as I can tell."

He shook his head. "She's not." He turned the phone over in his hand to look at the back. "Someone hexed your phone."

"What do you mean they hexed my phone?"

"They used their magic to filter out all pertinent information you might need for this case."

"Would that include text messages?" I asked, considering I hadn't gotten a response from Neve.

"Text messages, phone calls, app alerts," he said. "I'd bet it would include just about everything on here."

"What about photos?" I asked. "Those don't seem to be tampered with."

He navigated to my photos app. "Take a closer look at this one. Does it look the same as when you took it?" He showed me a picture of Randy dead in the kitchen.

Blood surrounded the body instead of water, and the knife in his chest was missing. "It's been altered."

He nodded.

"Can you fix it?" I asked. "How can I solve a case when I don't even have the proper photographs?"

He pressed the side buttons, then held down the power button until the phone went black. "I'll do my best."

When the screen flickered back on, a rainbow of colored lines filled the screen. He went through the same routine of pushing the buttons again.

This time when the screen came back on, it asked for my password like normal.

I typed it in as Xander averted his eyes. The moment the screen flashed to my home screen, the phone started dinging with messages.

Xander handed it to me. "Some of these may be private."

He'd probably seen Bernardo's name pop up. He didn't know Bernardo and I had decided just to be friends.

Sure enough, I had messages from Neve, the pictures were back to normal, and Xander's multiple voicemails came through.

As I played one, he pressed the pause icon on my screen. "You don't have to listen to them right now. In fact, why don't you just delete them now that I'm here and can tell you everything?"

There was no way I was deleting them.

I flipped over to the photos. "This looks more like what I remember." The water was back in the picture with Randy, as was the knife. "Do you think whoever did this to my phone was also the person who killed Randy and Gar?"

"I do. And that person had to have been magical."

27

After talking to my friends to make sure they were okay staying at least one more day, Xander and I headed back to the jamboree.

"I'll drive," I said when we got down to the empty valet stand. "Where is everyone?"

"Probably on break," Xander said. "My motorcycle is right over there. Let's just take it."

He handed me a helmet and helped me fasten the strap under my chin. When his knuckles grazed my neck, a burst of electricity exploded on my skin. His gaze shot up to mine.

Had he felt it too? Did he feel it every time we touched?

His big green eyes looked straight into my soul. Could he read my mind?

The fingers that had just been fixing the strap inched their way up my neck until they were entwined in my hair.

"You're so beautiful," he said. "I know we're not supposed to but—"

I didn't let him finish his sentence. I pushed up onto my tiptoes and pressed my lips to his.

If his motorcycle had exploded right next to us, it would have put out less heat than this kiss. My arms slipped beneath his leather jacket and wrapped around his rock-hard torso.

Xander was by far the best kisser I'd ever kissed.

He smiled when he pulled back, his hands still cupping my head. "Thank you. I've wanted to do that for so long."

I sighed as I dropped from my tiptoes. "We should probably go."

He kissed the tip of my nose. "There's so much I want to tell you."

I desperately wanted to hear every word he had for me, but there was a good possibility someone was out there trying to find and kill my mom while we stood in the parking lot making out.

"Soon," I said. "You can tell me soon."

He nodded and slipped on his own helmet.

I wrapped my arms tightly around his waist, savoring every bit of warmth he gave off as we drove out of the parking lot.

The ride was far too quick for my liking. I'd have happily sat on the back of his motorcycle all the way to Iowa.

When I handed him my helmet, he bent over and kissed me on the cheek. "Let's go take care of some business."

The way he trusted me to handle these situations without telling me to stay out of it and be careful meant more to me than he would ever know.

"Where do we start?" I asked.

"We go back to the crime scenes," Xander said. "We see if there are any magical traces left over."

"I thought you said the person wasn't killed magically," I said.

"That doesn't mean it couldn't have been a magical person who killed them in a non-magical way. Stranger things have happened."

He had a point.

Too bad there were no signs of magic at either of the crime scenes.

"They got this one cleaned up pretty quickly," Xander said when we returned to the front gates where Gar had died.

"Have you asked Emily—er—Miley if she can think of anyone who might want her hurt?"

Xander shook his head. "She doesn't know she might be in danger."

"But someone is protecting her, right?" I asked. "Or maybe several people with those tattoos."

"You keep mentioning these tattoos. What are you talking about? Something like a vine heart?"

"It's a heart with a vine wrapped around it," I said. "Almost twisted around it."

"And you've seen three people with this symbol tattooed on them?"

"Four, actually, and at least two had something to do with Miley. Her attorney and a big burly guy."

"The one who threatened you?"

"He told me to get away from where I was."

"Which was where?"

"I was watching the back of the motel where a secret ladder led to a secret entrance," I said.

"The back of the motel?" Xander, for once, seemed confused. "Why were you watching a secret entrance at the back of the motel?"

"Because that's where Miley was hiding from the police," I said. "Before she ended up turning herself in."

"Can you show it to me?"

"I don't know if I'll still be able to track her if she hasn't been there since before she turned herself in, but I'll show you where it was."

We walked out the gates and toward the motel. Our bodies were so close, our fingers brushed as our arms swung.

Finally, his fingers wound their way through mine. The sensation of sparks warmed me in the cool evening air.

"It's back here," I said, catching a glimpse of the door Xander had followed Miley and Eloise into earlier. "You looked pretty close with Eloise earlier."

"She's a great kid," Xander said. "Reminds me a lot of you."

"Do you know who her father is?" I asked.

"I don't," Xander said. "Miley's not super forthcoming with that."

Relief flooded me. At least he wasn't her dad.

I pointed up at the side of the building. "The door was up there, and the ladder came down right here. Andrea couldn't see it because I was the one who did the tracking, but she climbed up there with me."

"She's a good guardian. I'm glad you have her."

"Me too," I said.

"Can you see the door or the ladder anymore? If you try to track her again?"

I looked for the edges of magic, but nothing appeared. "Maybe it's been too long."

"Or maybe someone realized you'd been tracking her and did their own anti-tracking spell."

"Who could do that?" I asked. "Or is that something anyone can learn?"

I was still figuring out all the magical stuff, but Renée explained that some witches and warlocks had specific skills. Like I could heal and track. But there were also learnable types of magic.

"It's something you can learn," Xander said. "But few people have been able to acquire a license to do that. It's usually reserved for magical investigators."

My heart seemed to stop beating. "Your father," I said. "Maybe that's how he's kept everyone from finding my mother for so long. What if he used it recently? What if he's closer than we thought?"

"But if he used it to hide her, he's not the one trying to kill her."

"No, but maybe he knows who is," I said.

Xander started pacing. "How could I not have considered my father had a hand in all this? I mean, I don't think my father is a murderer, but he's done some pretty sketchy stuff in the past. And he doesn't believe in going through the appropriate channels."

"We need to find him," I said. "Does Miley know him in this life, or did he remove her memory and leave?"

"It's hard to tell," Xander said. "She's always been a very cautious person. I didn't want to push it too far, so I didn't ask many questions."

"And she knows nothing about magic, right?" I asked.

"No," Xander said. "She's completely unaware that magic exists."

"Does your dad have a tattoo like the one I've seen? Maybe he's part of that gang."

"I don't think he would have gotten a tattoo," Xander said. "Plus, he was always more of a lone wolf."

"Did you meet her attorney?" I asked, grasping at

straws, trying to connect any dots I could. "When you picked her up at the police station?"

"He'd already gone once I made it to the police station."

"Do you have a picture of your father you could show Miley?"

Xander pulled up his phone and navigated to his photo app. "Only from when I was a kid."

He showed me a photo of him, his father, and his mother.

His father was exactly how I remembered from when I'd gotten Mona.

"I think we need to ask her."

Xander sighed. "You're probably right."

We stood outside the motel room door. An invisible force field of protection held us back.

Xander mumbled a few words under his breath, and the heavy barrier fizzled out until he could knock on the door. I wanted to ask what it would have been like if Miley or Eloise had tried to leave, but we didn't have time for questions with long answers.

The door cracked, and when Eloise saw Xander, she threw it open wide and smiled. "I didn't think you were coming back tonight." Then her gaze transferred to me. "Who is that?"

"This is my friend, Ellie," Xander said.

"Did I hear you say Ellie?" Miley said, her voice sweet

and sassy in equal parts. "You finally brought her to meet us?"

Finally? They knew about me.

"She's in town working on the murder cases," Xander said, then turned to me. "I may have talked about you before."

Miley appeared in the doorway, her smile bright. She rested a hand on Eloise's shoulder as she looked me up and down. "May have talked about her? You can barely stop talking about her."

"It's honestly kind of annoying," Eloise said.

Miley laughed, then said, "Be nice."

Xander blushed.

"Plus, Ellie and I have already met," Miley said. "Unofficially."

"It's nice to meet you," I squeaked out.

"I'm Miley Mulroney, and this is my daughter, Eloise." Miley held out a hand for me to shake.

Her hand was warm and soft and I never wanted to let go.

After, I held my hand out for Eloise, but she crossed her arms over her chest.

"Eloise," Miley's voice was a gentle warning of manners.

"It's okay," I said. "She doesn't have to shake my hand. I am happy to meet you, though. I was looking for you when your mom got arrested."

"I can take care of myself," Eloise mumbled. "I don't need anyone looking out for me."

"Why don't you come in," Miley said, ignoring her

daughter. "Maybe I can help with the case. I knew Randy and Gar."

"That's exactly why we're here," I said, following Xander into the small hotel room. "I've spoken to several people, but I feel like I'm missing something. Do you have any thoughts about who the killer might be?"

"Probably one of the Three Musketeers," Miley said. "Bridget, Stacie, or KayLynn. Those three cannot be trusted."

"They're definitely on my suspect list."

Miley and Eloise sat on one of the queen-sized beds, Xander sat on the other, and I sat on the single worn desk chair.

"I'm glad they're on someone's suspect list," Miley said. "The police don't seem to think they're responsible."

"What makes you call them the Three Musketeers?"

"They're practically inseparable," Miley said. "Sure, they're always arguing, but I'm not buying that they didn't know about the others' relationships with Randy."

"But why would any of them kill Gar?"

"Maybe she caught one of them in the act of killing Randy," Miley said with a shrug.

I shook my head. "At least not as far as she told me. She said she saw you with him."

Miley gasped and looked at Eloise. "I most certainly was not with him. I promise."

Eloise rolled her eyes.

Miley ignored her and turned back to me. "Randy and I have a bit of a history. He and I dated about a year ago. I was pretty sad when it happened." She glanced at Eloise. "I never would have gone back to him."

Eloise's only reaction was a slight shrug.

"If I show you a picture of someone, do you think you could tell me if you've seen him before?" I asked, reaching for Xander's phone.

He handed me the photo of his family on the screen. I zoomed in so only his father's face was showing.

"I can try," Miley said. "I see a lot of people at the diner. I try to get to know the regulars, but I couldn't possibly know all the patrons."

I turned the phone toward her.

She reached out and took it from me, her eyes widening as she pivoted away from Eloise.

"Who is it?" Eloise asked, completely aware of our mother hiding the screen from her.

"Can we speak outside, please?" Miley stood from the bed and led Xander and me outside. "Eloise, you stay here."

Eloise objected, but the look Miley gave her had her stopping in her tracks.

"Where did you get this picture?" Miley whispered to Xander when the door was closed securely behind us.

"Who is it?" I asked. "Do you think this man could have killed one or both of them?"

Her eyes flooded with tears. "I don't know. I haven't seen him in almost ten years." She turned the phone toward us. "This is Eloise's biological father."

29

My head spun at the revelation. I reached out to grab Xander's arm.

"Now, tell me how *you* know him," Miley said. "Did he send you here? Are you going to help him take Eloise from me?"

From the look on Xander's face, he was just as shocked as Miley and me.

Eloise wasn't just my sister. She was Xander's too.

Did that mean he was my stepbrother?

No.

His dad wasn't married to my mom. We just shared a sister. That had nothing to do with our relationship.

Even as I said the words in my head, I knew they weren't true, and judging by the look on Xander's face, he was having similar revelations.

"I need some answers, and I need them now," Miley said in her stern mom voice.

Here I thought she and Xander were dating when she'd been with his father years before.

"That man is my father," Xander said, taking the phone back from Miley. "And now I need to find him."

Xander stormed away, leaving Miley and me staring after him.

"That's his father?" Miley finally asked though I wasn't sure she was even talking to me. "All this time?"

"I'm so sorry," I said.

"Do you think he killed them? Do you think he was trying to get to me? Or to Eloise?"

"Is there any reason you'd think he'd try to hurt you or Eloise?" I asked.

She shook her head. "He was never violent, and it only happened once. I woke up the next morning, and he was gone. But I've always worried he'd find out about her and come back asking for joint custody or something. I've heard some horrible stories of parents having to share their kids. I just can't imagine sharing her with anyone. She's my entire life."

The words were like knives stabbing into my chest and twisting simultaneously. Eloise was her world. Just like I should have been. I might have been if Xander's father hadn't gotten in the way.

"I'm going after him," I said. "Stay inside and lock the door."

Miley went back into the motel room and closed the door, the locks clicking into place.

I ran toward where Xander was putting on his helmet.

"Where are you going?" I asked.

"He's close. I can sense it," Xander said. "How could he do this? He's such a sleazebag. My poor mom."

He started his motorcycle, effectively ending the conversation.

"Teleport back to the hotel," Xander shouted. "Andrea will kill me if I leave you alone."

"I can come with you," I yelled over the rumbling engine sound.

He reached out and squeezed my hand. "This is something I need to do alone."

He dropped my hand and blazed off, shouting behind him, "Go back to the hotel."

I mumbled under my breath. "No."

"If he thinks he'll find me, he's sorely mistaken." A man who came out of nowhere started coughing behind me.

When I spun around, I knew instantly who it was. "Gerald."

He smiled. "You recognize my voice?"

I ignored his question. "Why are you here?" I reached for my phone to call Xander to come back.

"To talk to you, of course. Please don't call him," he said. "I had to wait until you were away from everyone else."

Here I'd thought I didn't need a guardian, but standing outside in the dark with a strange man made me anxious on a whole new level.

"I should probably go," I said, backing up like I would have if faced by a bear while hiking in the mountains. My hands shook so violently I had to shove them in my jacket pocket. There was no way I could focus well enough to teleport properly.

"You don't need to be afraid of me," Gerald said, stepping closer.

It took every bit of my gumption not to run away screaming. "What do you want to talk to me about?"

"Your mother," he said. "You didn't heed my warnings."

"I'm not going to tell her anything about the past."

"You don't think she sees the resemblance between the two of you? It's almost impossible to miss."

"She doesn't seem to," I said. "But you could do everyone a massive favor and just fix her memories. I know you're the only one who can."

He shook his head. "I won't be doing that."

"Because she knows something about you?" I narrowed my eyes. "And if she had her memories back, you could be in a world of hurt, right?"

"She'd become the next Grand Witch and would have no choice but to bring charges against me."

"Wouldn't being the Grand Witch give her the authority not to bring charges against you?"

"I don't expect you to understand," he said.

"Then explain it to me."

Another coughing fit took over his body, rendering him incapable of speaking.

"Or don't," I said. "But let's get on with this. I need to get back before someone notices I'm gone."

"They think you're with Xander, and Xander's too caught up in finding me to realize you didn't go back to the hotel like he told you to."

How long had he been standing there? Did he know he was Eloise's father?

"Did you kill Randy and Gar?"

"Why would I kill them?" He coughed again. "Come on. You're the investigator. What might my motivation be for wanting them dead?"

"I—well—I don't really know you. And I'm not exactly an investigator. I just help with crimes sometimes." I sounded like a child trying to explain how to solve a calculus problem using basic arithmetic. "Maybe you were trying to frame Miley, so she'd go to jail and couldn't spill your secret, even if she gained her memories back. Who would believe a murderer anyway, right?"

"What about Gar? She died while Miley was in jail. What would my motive have been there?"

"To get her out because you felt bad?"

"Trust me. If I framed someone, the evidence would have been so rock solid that person would never have seen the light of day again once they were arrested." He crossed his arms over his chest. "Randy's was a sloppy murder. Gar's was even sloppier."

"You think they were passion killings? Heat of the moment types?"

"Maybe." He shrugged. "But they had nothing to do with me. And they had nothing to do with Miley either. She was just in the wrong place at the wrong time."

"Then why are you here?"

"To keep you away from Miley," Gerald said. "Though, obviously, I've failed."

"But why? Why would you do that? Why would you steal my opportunity at a normal chance in life?"

"That's what you think I did?" He sighed. "How about I take you out for a drink or coffee? There's so much I need to tell you."

30

There was absolutely no way I was going anywhere with this man. "Why don't you just tell me right here?"

"Science has proven that talking over a warm beverage makes people more accepting of what's being talked about." He stepped away from me. "There's a coffee shop right around the corner up there. It's always busy, day and night, so there's no way I'll be able to hurt you. And I'll go first so you can have the upper hand."

This felt like a trap, but I couldn't prove it.

"I have to tell someone where I'll be," I said, pulling my phone from my satchel. "Would you rather that be Xander or Andrea?"

"Xander won't hear his phone with the noise of the motorcycle."

"Then I'll tell Andrea," I said.

"Fine by me, just don't use my name," he said. "She can meet us there, but she can't sit with us at the table. The information I have is for you and only you."

162

The fact that he was allowing me to call my guardian made me feel slightly better.

She answered on the first ring. "Ellie? Is everything okay?"

"I have a lead on the case," I said. "But Xander had to leave abruptly. Could you meet me at a coffee shop and just hang out at a separate table to ensure everything is on the up and up?"

The rustling of a jacket in the background gave me my answer before she did. "Just text me the address, and I'll be right there. I'm going to have Xander's head for leaving you alone."

I hung up and texted her the address.

"Everything good?" Gerald asked.

"Yep, go ahead."

He turned and started walking down the sidewalk toward downtown Denver. When he got far enough in front of me that I could run in the other direction and get to safety, I followed.

My phone lit up in my hand—a message from Neve.

When I opened it, I saw roughly ten to twelve other unread messages about the case. I scrolled to where the first one came in and started reading.

NEVE

The picture won't come through.

Are you sure this is the picture you sent?

Attached to that message was a screenshot of what looked like just a dark, grainy, nothing photo.

Did you say there was no blood, but there was a stab wound?

Ellie? Are you there?

Can you send me the picture again?

There wasn't blood at the first crime scene either, right? But there was water that might have washed it away?

Ellie. Please respond. You're freaking me out.

Do I need to come out there?

Is Xander there? Andrea?

Okay, I'm coming to Colorado.

Please be okay.

I hurriedly typed in a reply.

Just as I was about to hit send, a deep voice was in my ear. "Don't you know you shouldn't be on your phone while walking by yourself at night?"

One large arm wrapped around my torso while a hand clapped over my mouth.

My phone fell to the ground, its screen flickering off.

"Let me go," I tried to scream, but the words didn't go past the hand over my mouth.

I kicked and wiggled, but nothing worked. The man holding me was too strong.

I could see Gerald ahead of me, walking as if nothing was happening. Had he set this up? How could I have been so stupid not to be aware of my surroundings?

"Why are you still here? I thought I told you to leave," the man's voice was the same as when I'd been spying on Miley from the grass.

I didn't even try to reply since my voice wouldn't work.

What were my options? I willed my brain to think as quickly as possible.

I could teleport, but this guy would end up coming with me. I'd need to teleport somewhere where he'd either have to let me go or someone could help me.

The coffee shop.

Gerald would be there soon, and Andrea would already be there with any luck. Plus, if it were as busy as Gerald had said it would be, this guy would have no choice but to let me go.

I focused on the location, closed my eyes, and searched for the edges of magic.

"What are you doing?" the man asked. "Stop that."

I could feel fear flowing through him. And something else. Something different.

Just as I was about to disappear, he let go, and I teleported alone, landing smack dab in the coffee shop.

Several people screamed at the sight of me.

Two women at the table nearest me fell out of their chairs, their coffee spilling everywhere.

The barista dropped the metal carafe of milk she'd been steaming onto the floor as the steam machine sputtered, and she tried to get it to shut off.

"Where did you come from?" A man asked, looking up as if I'd dropped right through the ceiling.

"I've been here the whole time," I said, trying to talk my way out of the mess I'd created. Sure, it had been for a good cause, but all these people were looking at me the same way people had my entire life every time my hair would change—like I was some freak. "I just fell. Maybe you were too into your coffee and conversation to notice me."

I was a terrible liar, but people's minds seemed to fasten onto more logical explanations of things.

The sputter of the steam machine stopped, the people hushed, and the entire café was silent.

I was about to run out the door, but at that very moment, Gerald walked through the doors, and behind him, Andrea.

Gerald looked confused to see me there. He even glanced behind him, only to come face to face with Andrea.

She didn't acknowledge him, though. She didn't know who he was.

"Excuse me," she walked past him to get to me. "Are you okay?"

"Let's talk about it somewhere else," I said, acutely aware of all the eyes watching my every move.

She didn't need me to say anything else. She turned and marched back out of the coffee shop, clearing the way for me with her death glare.

When we were outside on the sidewalk, she turned back at me but then noticed that Gerald had followed us out. "Can I help you with something?"

"I'm here to talk to Ellie," Gerald said. "About the case."

"Right," Andrea said. "I'm, uh, just a friend."

"Nice to meet you," he said, then turned to me. "Now, can you please explain what just happened in there?"

I agreed to explain once we'd found another coffee shop. Being as we were in downtown Denver, it wasn't hard to find one only a block away.

Andrea sat at a table close to the front door while I ordered the two of us coffees.

Gerald ordered his after mine.

After delivering Andrea's coffee, I joined Gerald in a secluded booth at the back of the coffee shop.

I took the seat facing the door and Andrea so I could signal her if I needed help. Not that I thought I would, but the night had already thrown me more curveballs than I was used to.

"Ready to tell me?" Gerald asked.

"You first," I said.

He shifted in his seat. "Fine. Let's start at the beginning."

I wrapped my hands around my mug to ease my anxious energy.

"As you've probably already figured out, your mother

comes from a very powerful family. The Vanderwicks have been Grand Witches for centuries and have done a wonderful job of it. When Esme—your grandmother— became pregnant with your mother, she didn't know what she was getting into with your grandfather."

"I wouldn't exactly call him my grandfather," I said.

"The man who is biologically your grandfather," he corrected. "He had one goal in life—to create a male heir."

"Right, so he impregnated a bunch of witches and ended up with a bunch of daughters."

"Until Monroe."

"Until Monroe." I nodded, then took a sip of my coffee.

"Who had decided that the entirety of his father's money should go to him. But to do that, he had to—"

"Kill all the other heirs, right?" I said. "I already know all of this."

"You do?" He seemed genuinely confused.

"Harriet, my cousin and Ambeline Nightingale's daughter, has been looking for him for years. She found me and told me everything you're telling me now."

"All right." He considered this for a moment. "Ambeline was the one who warned your mother that Monroe was trying to kill everyone off. Ambeline wanted Emily to join her to fight Monroe. But Emily had just found out she was with child."

"Me."

"You," he confirmed. "She was so in love with you from the moment she knew. But as Ambeline told her more about Monroe, she knew she had to protect you. So she came to me."

"Why?"

"Why what?"

"Why would she go to you? Surely, she knew other witches who could help her. Why would she go to you? Did she know you?"

"She knew of me," Gerald said. "She was next in line to be Grand Witch, and my family has always been on the council. Plus, I've made a name for myself in the magical business."

"What kind of name?"

"A name that Xander would consider unethical, but that's just because he's too big a rule follower. Sometimes rules need to be broken to help people in need."

"Like my mother."

"Erasing someone's memory is not technically something the council or the Grand Witch believes we should do, but sometimes it's necessary."

"So, she went to you, and you formulated a plan?"

He shook his head. "She had the plan all figured out. Your mother is an amazing woman."

My protective instincts made me want to leap across the table and shake him for impregnating her and leaving her when he had a wife and family, but I'd never betray Emily like that.

"What did her plan entail?"

He pulled a document out of his jacket pocket and laid it on the table. "I figured you'd have to see it to believe it."

I skimmed over what looked like a handwritten plan and contract, four pages front and back. "This is a lot."

"She thought of everything," he said.

"Everything except how much this decision would affect my life."

"No, she thought of that, too." He sipped his coffee. "But I don't think we could have guessed how strong your magic would be. Admittedly, even though she loved you, she was young and knew little about being a mother. I don't think she would have imagined you ending up in so many foster homes. On the back of the third page, you'll find the clause that says I could not have contact with you because if anyone saw us together, they might have figured out who you were."

I didn't flip to the back of the third page. I'd read the entire thing later when I was alone and had time to process it. "But you did have contact with me. You gave me Mona."

He shrugged. "So I broke the rules a bit. How was she to know? She didn't even remember making the contract. And you needed Mona. It was the only way I could help you at that moment."

"Risky," I said.

"Everything was going fine until Xander found out about you," he said. "I mean, he'd seen you several times in his life as I checked in on you from time to time. But when you were about seventeen, Xander found this contract. He was newly appointed to the council and was ready to turn me in until I told him more about you. That's when he started as your guardian."

"When I was seventeen?" I'd been so angry that he was my guardian. I never thought to ask when that had come to be. Which meant Xander was likely the one who had set up the pho restaurant for me. Tears of thanks welled in my eyes.

"He's a great guardian." Gerald's face beamed with pride. "He watched you like a starving man watches the dumpster behind a pizzeria. I think he felt obligated to fix what he saw as a misstep on my part. Eventually, he found Cliff Haven and your grandmother and told her about you. But he was too late."

I gripped my coffee so tightly that my knuckles were white. "She died before I could get there."

Gerald nodded. "I don't think Xander will ever forgive himself for that. And at that moment, he knew he had to find your mother. He had to give you at least one of your family members back."

32

What about my father?

The question was on the tip of my tongue, but I couldn't ask. What if he said he was my father?

But that wouldn't line up, would it? Emily sought him out after she found out she was pregnant with me, right?

"I know you have questions I can't answer," Gerald said as if reading my mind. "It's part of the contract that if I were to = come into contact with you, I wouldn't give you any information that would disrupt the spell."

"What about the information you just gave me? Could it disrupt the spell?"

"I've told you all that I can. But you needed to know before you tried anything stupid," he said. "From what I've observed, your magic is powerful enough to break any spell I've ever cast. But if you do, it could have disastrous consequences."

"Then you need to do it."

"I can't."

"Why not?"

"Because it's in the contract."

"You've broken the contract before."

"Only to help you."

"Giving me my mother back would help me."

"Maybe." He sat back, and his coughing fit returned.

He reached for his coffee mug, but it was empty.

I stood and asked the barista for a glass of water.

Once I had it, I held it just out of his reach. "I'll give you the water if you undo the spell."

He laughed and dropped his outstretched hand, still coughing.

A groan escaped my lips as I set the water on the table in front of him and returned to my seat.

He sucked the entire glass of water down within seconds, effectively stopping his coughing.

"I'll deal with my mother if she wants to turn you in for whatever it is," I said. "I'll convince her not to."

Gerald shook his head. "Too much has changed. Too many people will be affected."

"Who else?" I asked. "Who else will be affected? You, me, Emily, and who?"

"People I can't tell you right now."

"Then I think this conversation is over," I said, taking the papers in front of me and standing. "If you're unwilling to help, I'll have to find someone who is."

"What does that mean?" He stood and followed me toward the door.

"You can't possibly be the only one who knows how to do this spell or break it. I am about to be the Grand Witch of the States. I'm sure Renée will help me find someone willing to help." I was bluffing because Renée most likely would not let me find someone who did illegal magic.

"No one can take my spell away without doing damage."

I whipped around to face him, and he almost ran straight into me. "Not even you?"

He glanced down at his feet.

"Look at me."

His gaze met mine.

"Can you reverse the spell without damaging her mind?"

He hesitated. "I can, but I won't."

I wanted to strangle him, but that would do me no good. I needed to figure out how to get him to reverse the spell.

He pushed past me and walked out of the coffee shop.

Andrea stood, but I motioned for her to sit back down. I took the seat across from her. "He's completely useless."

"How is he related to the case?"

I glanced out the door to make sure Gerald was gone. The last thing I needed was Andrea turning him in to the magical authorities.

"Don't be mad. But he has nothing to do with the case. That was Xander's father," I said.

Andrea stood and started toward the door, but I grabbed her arm and pulled her back into her chair.

"He's gone," I said.

"Why didn't you tell me?" she asked. "He's a wanted man."

"He's also the only person who can take the spell off

my mother. And I'm sure if we send him to magical prison, he won't do that."

"Did he say he'd do it without going to jail?" Andrea asked, crossing her arms over her chest and raising her eyebrows, waiting for my reply.

"Well, no."

She shook her head. "You should have told me."

"Do you want to know what he told me?" I asked.

She said nothing at first, but then her shoulders drooped, and she dropped her arms. "Okay, yes. I want to know."

I was about to reply, but three loud, intoxicated women walked through the doors.

"Aren't those the truck drivers who might have killed Randy and Gar?"

I looked more closely. She was right. Bridget, Stacie, and KayLynn giggled all the way up to the register. KayLynn did the ordering, as she seemed to be sober or the least drunk of the three.

"Why are they together?" Andrea asked. "I thought they hated each other."

"Except Miley just called them the Three Musketeers. She said they fought, but they were almost always together."

"But they wouldn't have been together when they were all sleeping with the same dude."

"Or would they?" I asked with a laugh.

She smiled. "I mean, I guess it's possible."

I shook my head. "To each their own."

"You should go over there and try to talk to them

again," Andrea said. "Alcohol can override our brain-to-mouth filters, you know?"

I stood from the table. "Let's hope so."

"I'll be here if you need anything."

As I approached the booth with the three women, a man slipped into the open seat next to a giggling Bridget.

"What's your name?" Stacie purred.

The man mumbled something I couldn't hear.

"You're cute," Bridget said, petting the man's long, wavy hair. "Do you have a girlfriend? Not that any of us care, apparently."

Bridget and Stacie started cackling.

KayLynn looked like she might pass out on the table from exhaustion.

I desperately wanted to spy on them, but if they saw me, they'd shut down anything they might be ready to tell this mystery man.

When I passed their booth, I turned to look away from them. The bathroom door was just down the hall past their booth. I ducked inside so anyone watching me wouldn't be suspicious.

The bathroom was empty, and I didn't hear anyone in the hallway.

I crouched down and cracked the door open, but the door opened too easily. Before I could get out of the way, someone barreled in, slamming the door into my face, and sending me flat on my back.

"What in the heavens are you doing down there?" Neve stood over me. "I should kill you right now for making me think you were dead."

33

"How did you—how are you—where—why—"

"Did I knock the sense out of you?" Neve asked. She wore khaki shorts and a light blue tank top.

I took her outstretched hand and stood. "How did you know I was here?"

"I called every hotel in the Denver Metro area until I found where you were staying. Your friends knew where you were."

"That must have taken forever."

"Do you know how long the drive is from the middle of Iowa to Denver, Colorado? Like a million hours. I had plenty of time."

"I'm so sorry," I said. "I should have called you, but I didn't know my phone had been hexed. Then it shattered, and I had to leave it behind when I teleported to get away from the guy who keeps threatening me if I don't leave."

My mind went to the photos I hadn't uploaded to the

cloud, and tears welled in my eyes. "I think I lost all my pictures."

"We'll figure out a way to get them back," Neve said. "Where is your guardian?"

"Out there," I said. "I came in here to listen to the women in the booth out there. They're my prime suspects."

"Randy was killed in one of three ways—stabbing, poison, or suffocation."

"Right," I said. "I got that text message."

"But when you sent me the photo of Gar, it was all wonky, so I called my friend who works for Denver PD, and they said Gar was killed in the same three ways."

"All three?"

"All three." She nodded. "This is one of the first cases I've seen where someone used multiple methods to kill the suspect."

"Why?" I asked. "Why would they use three methods?"

"The poison may not have been working fast enough. Stabbing is much more intense than people think, and the suffocation could have been a last-ditch effort to end it all."

"So, technically, they would have died of suffocation, right?"

"There's no way to tell," she said. "But we know the stab wounds on the two victims don't match up. One was made by someone who was left-handed, and one was by someone who was right-handed."

"Or one ambidextrous person," I offered.

She moved her head from side to side as if she was considering it. "I suppose that's possible."

"Were the poisons the same?"

"Yes," she said. "But the stomach contents weren't. Randy's had freshly eaten pancakes and coffee in his stomach. Gar had an almost empty stomach besides copious amounts of red wine."

"And the suffocation?" I asked.

"Someone very strong suffocated Randy, whereas the suffocation marks on Gar's face were much less noticeable and were probably only done to create the same look on the second victim as on the first."

"You think two different people did this," I said.

"I'm almost certain of it."

The bathroom door opened, and a young woman I'd never seen before walked in and took the farthest stall of the two.

"Anything else?" I whispered.

"The victims weren't killed where their bodies were found," Neve said.

"I suspected as much," I said. "Mostly because of the lack of blood from the stab wound."

"That's one part of it," she said. "But the other part comes from the rug burns and embedded fibers."

"Embedded where?"

"In their skin." Neve stopped talking when the woman came out of the stall.

"Are you guys okay?" the woman asked after she washed her hands and turned around to get a paper towel from the wall where we stood.

"We're fine," Neve said. "Thanks."

She was dressed much fancier than anyone else in the coffee shop, with a tight black minidress and strappy shoes.

"Hey, can I ask you a question?" Before she could walk out the bathroom door, I stepped in front of her. "What does that tattoo on your foot mean?"

She had the heart and vine tattoo, and I was tired of guessing its meaning.

"Wouldn't you like to know?" She threw her long dark hair over her shoulder and tried to walk past me with more attitude than anyone needed.

I blocked her path. "I need to know."

Before I could react, she pushed me hard to the side, knocking me into the sink while she darted out of the bathroom.

I righted myself and took off after her.

She was at the door when I burst from the bathroom door.

Andrea was looking at me, and I pointed to the woman who had just run outside. Andrea got the hint and ran after her.

On my way, I realized my three suspects had left, as had the man speaking with them.

By the time I made it outside, Andrea was nowhere in sight.

Neve was right behind me. "Where'd they go?"

"I don't know," I said. "The suspects are gone, and Andrea chased after the woman in the bathroom."

"What was all that about a tattoo?"

"Several people have tried to thwart my plans here,

and all of them had a tattoo with a heart and a vine wrapped around it. Does that ring any bells for you?"

"The only symbol I've ever seen like that was at a diner I visited once when I went skiing a couple of years ago," she said. "The menus had the symbol on them. Maybe it was a logo of some sort?"

When she mentioned a diner, my insides clenched. I described the diner I'd seen in the mural.

"That's right. You're from here. You've probably been there before. They had the most delicious pancakes, even better than the ones at Katie's Café."

"With crispy edges," I said. "I never technically visited the diner, but I think that's where my mother's been this entire time."

"Wait, you found your mother?"

I didn't have time to explain anything else. Andrea was walking back toward us, dragging the young woman back with her.

34

Andrea and the young woman in strappy heels, a tight black minidress, and long, dark hair stopped in front of Neve and me.

"Why did I need to chase her down?" Andrea asked.

"I needed to ask her a question, and when I did, she ran."

Andrea's expression faltered as if that wasn't exactly the crime she thought this woman had committed.

"Well then, ask."

The woman struggled, but Andrea was stronger.

"What does your tattoo mean?" I asked, pointing at her foot.

"What tattoo?" The young woman asked.

"The heart one on your—" The tattoo was gone. "How is that possible? You had the tattoo in the bathroom."

"What bathroom? I didn't see you in any bathroom. You must have me confused with someone else."

"Uh, no," Neve said. "I saw you too. It was definitely you."

"But she had a tattoo," I said. "Was it washable? Did you wash it off?"

"She couldn't have," Andrea said. "I never lost sight of her. She wouldn't have had time."

Frustration bubbled up inside me. "Just let her go."

Andrea did with an apologetic look, then turned her attention to me.

When I was the only one looking at the young woman, she smirked, stuck her tongue out at me, and darted into the night.

"Did you see that?" I pointed after her. "It was her. Maybe she's magical. Does she have magic that I can't see?"

"She's not a witch," Andrea said. "I would have known. I think you need to get some rest. We can go back to the investigation tomorrow."

I wanted to object, but I couldn't. She was right. I was exhausted.

The smell of coffee pulled me out of bed the next morning. When I walked down the stairs, all my friends, including Neve, Penelope, and Andrea, sat around the large table chatting like they'd known each other their entire lives.

I couldn't help but stop and watch them with a smile on my face. They were all here for me, but it was wonderful to see them enjoying themselves.

"Ellie, get over here and have some coffee," Katie

stood from the table and poured me a cup. "Andrea and Neve were just catching us up from last night."

"Ugh," I said. "Last night was a mess, but I think today will be better."

"How'd you sleep?" Nancy asked.

"I slept great," I said. "Better than I thought I could have."

They all giggled.

"What?" I asked, realizing I'd been left out of a joke.

"Andrea may have sprinkled a little sleepy dust on the penthouse last night," Amy said. "It seems we all had the best night's rest with the best dreams we've had in a long time."

"It was just a touch to encourage good sleep," Andrea said. "I didn't do a sleeping spell or anything."

Just the fact that she knew how to do a sleeping spell was both awesome and intimidating.

"Well, it helped. So, thank you."

"To Andrea," Fran said, holding up her coffee cup.

"Here, here," we all replied, clinking our mugs together.

"Mmmm," I said. "Katie, you make the best coffee."

"No magic required," Katie said with a wink.

"What's the plan for today?" Nancy asked. "Do you think we'll solve the case?"

My stomach clenched. "I don't know. I hope so."

"Where did Xander run off to last night?" Katie asked. "I figured he'd at least drop you off after you went off on your date."

"It wasn't a date," I said, feeling the warmth creep up

my neck. "We had to go chat with some people about the murders. Then he went to keep looking for his dad."

"So he can break the spell, and your mom will regain her memories?" Amy asked.

"Something like that," I said. "But I think it'll be pretty hard convincing his dad to do it even if Xander finds him."

"Don't lose hope," Katie said, placing a hand over mine and squeezing. "We'll get our Emily back. I just know it."

"We should probably head over to the jamboree," Andrea said. "We can get you some of Miley's pancakes and see if Xander went back last night."

"And we have more to discuss about the case," Neve said. "We were interrupted last night, but I have more to tell you."

I nodded. "You guys don't have to come with me if you don't want to."

"Are you kidding?" Fran asked. "I have to see who gets the trophy for the best truck."

"Do you think they'll still hand them out now that both event owners are dead?" Nancy asked.

I hadn't even considered that possibility. "Hopefully, one of the volunteers will do it in their honor."

"Only one way to find out," Katie said, standing. "Let's get ready and get down there."

Mona was happy to take us to the jamboree. It seemed her time in the valet lot wasn't as exciting as our penthouse. She was probably mad that we'd left the magical hotel.

"I don't tell you this enough," I whispered as I clutched her metal wheel. "But thank you, Mona."

The wheel warmed beneath my touch.

Someone once told me that Mona's magic was only an extension of mine, but I knew that couldn't be true. Mona was her own little magical being. Maybe no one else would understand, but I did.

"Um, that's not good," Andrea said, pointing to the closed event gates.

"There's a sign," Nancy said, leaning forward between Andrea and me to see better through the windshield. "Get closer."

The sign on the gate said:

The Jubilant Jewel Jamboree has been canceled.

35

"It's canceled?" Fran asked from the back of Mona. "But the trucks are all still in there."

"It looks like they're packing up and leaving," Katie said. "And the food vendor stalls are empty."

Meaning, Miley and Eloise were probably gone too.

"There has to be another way in," I said. "I have to figure out who killed Gar and Randy. Why wouldn't the police require it to stay open? Wasn't this still an open investigation?"

Neve cleared her throat from the very back of the van. "I wanted to talk to you about that in private, but now is probably just as good a time as any."

Everyone turned to face her.

"The police are shelving the case for now. They don't have enough evidence to charge anyone."

"What!?" Everyone in the van started talking over one another.

When a whistle pierced the air, I expected to see

someone with fingers in their mouth, but no one seemed to be responsible.

Then another burst of whistle sound came from right next to me. Penelope.

"Thanks," I said, patting her back. "Okay, we need to keep our heads about us. The trucks are still in there. They haven't left yet. Let's get in there and figure out who did this."

"But the police—" Amy said.

"Nope," I said. "Right now, we're not going to worry about the police. We need to get evidence showing them that these were, in fact, murders."

"There's only one problem with that," Katie said. "There's a massive lock on that gate."

"Do you think you can use magic to unlock it?" Nancy asked.

"I don't think we need to," I said. "The trucks have to exit somehow. We'll just go in that way."

"Smart," Nancy said. "Then we won't leave any evidence that we were here."

"Are you planning on committing a crime?" Fran asked.

"No." Nancy gasped.

"Then who cares if there's evidence that we're here?" Fran said.

"If we break through a gate, that would be a crime," Nancy said in her duh voice.

Fran didn't reply.

"Mona, could you please find us another entrance?" I asked.

It took her less than a minute to find where the trucks were exiting.

"I hope we're not too late," Andrea said.

"We only need to talk to three people," I said. "And after the night of partying they had last night, I'd be willing to guess they're all still sleeping. At least, I hope so."

Many of the trucks had gone, but when we reached the row with KayLynn, Stacie, and Bridget's trucks, they were all still there.

"Let's split up," I said. "I'll take Stacie's."

"I'll come with you," Andrea said.

"Me too," Neve agreed.

"I'll take Bridget," Fran said, then looked at Amy. "Wanna join?"

"I'm in," Amy said with a nod.

"I guess that leaves us with KayLynn," Katie said to Nancy.

"Good, go in pairs," I said. "One person in each group should turn on their recording app on their phone while the other has 9-1-1 dialed and ready to press the call button. That way, we'll have a recording if anything happens, and the police will be on their way."

Nods came from all around.

The women piled out of the van and spread out.

I led the way as Neve, Andrea, and Penelope followed behind toward Stacie's truck-camper-car hauler thing.

I knocked on the door with steps on the sleeping part —the same way I'd gotten in the first time I'd visited.

Footsteps approached, and the door swung open.

I expected to see Stacie, but KayLynn stood at the top of the steps.

"Hey," I said. "Can I come in?"

"Bridget and Stacie are sleeping. And I—" She didn't finish her sentence before running toward the back of the trailer. The sound of vomiting came from the bathroom.

"I think she said we could come in, right?" Neve asked Andrea and me.

"That's what I heard," Andrea said with a smile.

"All right," I said. "Let's go in."

Stacie was in the big bed at the back of the trailer, while Bridget was on the loft bed above the truck cab. They had transformed the table that had been there before into another bed, where I suspected KayLynn had slept.

"You okay in there?" I asked loudly enough to wake the other two women.

"Stop shouting." Bridget moaned. "My head is on fire."

"Remind me never to drink red wine again," Stacie said from the back.

KayLynn vomited again as if agreeing.

"They drank a lot," Neve said, pointing to a trash bin overflowing with what looked like at least six wine bottles. "Do you think they shared it with anyone else?"

"No, it was just us," KayLynn said, emerging from the bathroom. "No one else."

I narrowed my eyes at her. "Except you weren't drunk last night like the other two."

"Yes, I was. How would you know?"

"I saw you at the coffee shop early this morning," I said. "You were perfectly coherent. Tired, but not drunk."

"There's no way two people drank all that wine," Neve said. "They'd be dead."

"What about that guy you were with last night?" I asked.

"The creepy one at the coffee shop?" Stacie sat up, clutching her head in her hands. "He went to the bathroom, and we bolted." She looked around her truck with a horrified expression, stood, and started cleaning.

I glanced down at the carpet to find a big red stain. "Well, here's where some of it went."

"Oh yeah." KayLynn's eyes widened as she hurried over and started scrubbing the spot with a random towel lying on the floor. "Bridget did that."

"I did not," Bridget said. "I'd never waste good wine by spilling it."

Neve knelt next to KayLynn. "That's not wine. It's blood."

36

"You're insane," Stacie said, moving to help KayLynn clean the stain. "It's not blood. It's wine. You should get out of my truck before I call the police."

"Be my guest," I said. "I'm sure they'd love to find the actual crime scene where you murdered Randy and Gar."

Stacie gasped. "We didn't kill anyone."

"Yes, you did. All of you. Together." The pieces were clicking into place in my mind. "You're smart. Using several methods really threw the police."

Bridget climbed down from the loft, nearly toppling over as she reached the bottom step. "You don't know what you're talking about."

"KayLynn?" I asked. "Do you want to say anything?"

KayLynn continued scrubbing silently as tears fell from her eyes onto the carpet.

"Okay, that's fine," I said. "Let me take a stab at it."

Neve winced at my pun.

"Sorry, too soon," I said. "My guess is that one of you

poisoned Randy's coffee when you saw him eating with Gar. Jealousy sucks, doesn't it?"

No one spoke.

"But the poison didn't kick in fast enough, and you panicked," I said. "So, Stacie, you invited him to come to your trailer. And, being a man, he took you up on the offer. Too bad when he got here, someone stabbed him. My guess is it was Bridget, but seeing as how both Bridget and KayLynn are right-handed, it could have been either of you."

KayLynn gagged and vomited all over the floor before rushing back to the bathroom.

Bridget steadied herself in the kitchen area as she gagged over the sink.

Stacie didn't even react as she continued scrubbing like her life depended on it.

"Stabbing is hard, though, isn't it?" I said. "And after one stab, Stacie realized how wrong she'd been in bringing him to her trailer. Not only because she's a complete clean freak and the blood from a stab wound would sully her perfect home on wheels, but also because carpet is tough to clean."

"So, you suffocated him," Neve said. "And seeing as how you look like the strongest physically, that's what ended up finishing him off."

"The three of you then dragged him out of the truck and set it up to look like he was killed in Miley's kitchen. You even took one of the knives from there and put it into the wound. The water was a nice touch to wash away some of the evidence, but leaving the knife in his chest was a huge mistake. The medical examiner could tell the knife wasn't the real murder weapon. And I'd venture to guess if I look in your pristinely organized drawers, I'd find a knife that matches with traces of blood on it."

Stacie looked up at me with wide eyes. "Fine, look, we didn't poison him. None of this was our idea. Gar did it."

"Funny how the only one who can't speak for herself is the one you'd blame. The only problem is, she's dead, too."

"She wouldn't be dead if she had stuck with the plan," Bridget said, her words slurring.

"Bridget, shut up," KayLynn yelled from the bathroom before vomiting again.

"Let's say Gar was responsible," I said. "Tell me how you ended up roped into all this."

"Gar found out he was sleeping with all of us before any of us knew," Stacie said. "She poisoned his coffee at breakfast, but when he wasn't dying, she panicked and dragged us into it."

"She came pounding on our doors in the middle of the night telling us Randy was cheating on all of us and this was our chance to get back at him. We just had to help her finish the job," Bridget said.

"And you just went along with it?" Andrea asked.

"We were mad," Stacie said. "And she told us it wasn't like we were actually killing him. She'd already done that with the poison that would eventually kill him, anyway."

"You didn't consider telling her she was a crazy person and calling an ambulance to save his life?" Neve asked.

No one spoke up.

"There was more to it, wasn't there?" I asked. "Gar

told you she'd split his life insurance money, right? Since all of you had a part in his life, you all deserved a piece."

"Well, we did," Bridget said.

"Bridget, shut up," KayLynn said, coming out of the bathroom.

"They're not cops," Bridget said. "They're just random people."

"But then when you were celebrating with copious amounts of wine," I said. "Gar changed her mind, right? Either she said she wouldn't give you the money, or she was going to go to the police with the information that the three of you killed him."

"She was always a—" KayLynn started.

Andrea interrupted, "There's no need for name-calling."

"Well, she was," KayLynn said. "But none of this is on me. I didn't do any of it."

"Have you ever heard the term guilty by association?" Stacie spat.

"I'll flip on you, and my testimony will keep me out of jail," KayLynn said.

"That's just like you," Bridget said. "You never were a team player."

"You killed my best friend and the father of my child," KayLynn shouted.

"The father of your child?" Stacie asked, coming to a stand. "What do you mean, the father of your child?"

KayLynn's hand went to her stomach.

"That's why you weren't drinking," I said.

"And why you've been barfing so much," Neve said.

"You were going to have a baby with my fiancé?" Stacie lunged at KayLynn.

"And my baby is going to inherit everything." KayLynn tried to fight her off, but Stacie was stronger.

Thankfully, Andrea jumped in and pulled Stacie off her.

"Are the police here yet?" Andrea asked.

Neve peeked out the door. "Looks like they're right on time."

The scary officer from the first day we'd been at the jamboree marched in and, after listening to the recording, arrested Stacie while two other officers detained the other two.

The trailer was way too small for nine of us.

I stepped outside as the officers read the women their rights.

"I waive my rights," KayLynn said. "I'll tell you everything if you don't send me to jail. I'll testify. I'm pregnant. I can't have my baby in jail."

"You'll need to speak to the district attorney about a deal," the scary officer said.

"Wow," Neve said when the three women were locked up in the police cars. "I'm impressed. How did you figure that out?"

"It's kind of like a dam breaking," I said. "Usually, I'll solve one little thing, and it's like a crack, but then everything else starts clicking into place and ends up bringing the whole dam down."

"That's amazing," Neve said.

"I agree," Xander said, walking out from behind the front of the truck. "She is amazing."

Neve disappeared pretty quickly once the police arrived. She said she needed to get back to Iowa so she wouldn't be fired, but there was no way Jake would fire her. She was way too good at what she did.

Katie and the gang gave Xander and me some space to talk while Andrea transferred the audio file from her phone to send to the police.

"I am so sorry I left you the way I did last night," he said. "I was so angry. I didn't use my head, which could have put you in danger."

"I saw your father," I said. "He knows you're looking for him."

"I know," Xander said. "I found him. He told me everything."

"I don't think he knows about Eloise."

"Me neither. And it's not my story to tell." Xander reached for my hand. "I know it's weird that we share a sister, but my father assures me there's no way he could be your father. I did a truth spell, and he told me he only cheated on my mother once with Emily."

It still grossed me out that Xander's dad had been with my mom, but at least there was no chance that Xander and I were related.

"Where is Emily?" I asked.

"She and Eloise are back at the diner," he said.

"Will you take me there?"

Xander squeezed my hands and smiled. "I'd love to. But first, there's something we need to do."

I glanced around. Everything had been solved here. "What about Katie and everyone?"

"Do you think Mona would let Andrea drive them home?"

"I don't know that Andrea will trust you with me," I said.

She'd looked at us no less than fifty times since we started talking.

"I'll talk to her," he said. "But this is important."

I nodded. "Then, of course."

He bent forward and kissed me on the cheek before he squeezed my hand and headed over to Andrea.

As I looked past them, Katie, Nancy, Fran, and Amy were all grinning from ear to ear while giving me thumbs-up signals.

Even Penelope didn't seem mad that Xander and I had been so close.

When Xander stopped his motorcycle in front of a hospital, my heart nearly stopped in my chest. "Why are we here?"

"My father is sick," he said, taking my helmet. "Something is wrong with his lungs. The doctors don't think he'll make it much longer. I wanted you to visit with him one more time to see if he'd reverse the spell since he wouldn't be alive to see the repercussions of it, anyway."

That would explain the coughing, but he had to have known he was sick before, and he'd still been unwilling to reverse the spell.

We walked through the doors, and Xander led me up a flight of stairs and down a hall to a dark corner room.

Gerald sat up in bed when we walked in and started coughing violently.

Xander handed his father the water from the table next to his bed.

He drank tiny sips until the coughing stopped. "I think I overdid it last night trying to talk to you."

"I'm so sorry you're going through this," I said. "If I had known, I wouldn't have made you walk outside in the cold."

"Don't blame yourself," he said. "I didn't know I was as bad as I am. Last night, when Xander caught up with me, it was only because I couldn't stop coughing, which meant I couldn't grasp my magic."

Panic flooded me. If he couldn't grasp his magic to get away from Xander, how would he use his magic to reverse the intricate, complicated spell he put on my mother?

There was only one option.

"I can heal you," I said.

Xander's eyes widened. "No—that's not—I did not bring you here for that."

"I know you didn't," I said. "But it's the only way."

"I don't deserve the healing," Gerald said.

"Maybe that's true, but I deserve my mother." My eyes clouded with tears. "I won't do it without your permission."

He looked at Xander.

"Only on one condition," Xander said. "You must make a magically binding promise to reverse the spell after she heals you. And not years after, months, weeks, or days. We'll give you time to ensure you have the energy to complete the reversal without any damage to anyone involved. Also, no trickery or loopholes allowed. If there's something you'll be in trouble for because Emily remembers, then so be it. We'll figure that out later."

Gerald looked from Xander to me and back again.

Xander shifted his weight from one foot to another and held a hand out for his father. "Do we have a deal?"

***

Want to find out what Gerald says? Figure out what the deal is with that tattoo? Or just see what happens with Ellie and Xander?

You don't have to wait long for the answers to these questions and many others!

. . .

Cosmic Conspiracy—Book 8 in the Magical Mane Mystery Series—releases in early 2023. Preorder it now!

ACKNOWLEDGMENTS

A massive thanks goes to my family, friends, and God. Without you, there would be no books.

Thank you to my writing friends. Whether it's our daily messages, our zoom sprints, or seeing each other at conferences, I am so thankful for your friendship and support.

My readers are the absolute best. Without my readers, I'd be out of a job. Thank YOU so much for reading my books —I hope they have given you a bit of escape and joy.

A huge thanks to my beta readers, ARC readers, social media sharers, and fellow authors. You are all integral to my success.

ABOUT THE AUTHOR

Stella Bixby is a native Coloradan who loves to snowboard, pluck at the guitar, and play board games with her family. She was once a volunteer firefighter and a park ranger, but now spends most of her time making up stories and trying to figure out what to cook for dinner.

Connect with Stella on Facebook, Twitter, and Instagram @StellaBixby.

Stella loves to hear from her readers!
www.stellabixby.com

Spelunking Speculations: Book 5

Festival Fiasco: Book 6

Jamboree Justice: Book 7

Cosmic Conspiracy: Book 8